NEVERLAND

Neverland

FABLED PLACES
AND FABULOUS VOYAGES
OF HISTORY AND LEGEND

STEVEN FRIMMER

THE VIKING PRESS   NEW YORK

PICTURE CREDITS

The Bobbs-Merrill Company, Inc., and Thomas Nelson & Sons, Ltd.,
p. 141

Map Division, The New York Public Library, Astor, Lenox and Tilden
Foundations: pp. 6, 14, 88, 116, 184

The New York Public Library Picture Collection: pp. 24, 36, 46, 49, 56,
58–59, 71, 77, 81, 85, 92, 98, 99, 101, 103, 128, 156, 161, 192, 199

Maps on pp. 29, 39, 51, 65, by Rafael Palacios

FIRST EDITION

Copyright © Steven Frimmer, 1976
All rights reserved
First published in 1976 by The Viking Press
625 Madison Avenue, New York, N.Y. 10022
Published simultaneously in Canada by
The Macmillan Company of Canada Limited
Printed in U.S.A.

1 2 3 4 5 80 79 78 77 76

Library of Congress Cataloging in Publication Data
Frimmer, Steven.   Neverland: fabled places
and fabulous voyages of history and legend.
Bibliography: p.   Includes index.
1. Geographical myths—Juvenile literature.   2. Voyages
and travels—History—Juvenile literature.   I.   Title.
GR940.F75   398'.42   76–26894
ISBN 0–670–50625–7

FOR GRACE AND IS

CONTENTS

PART ONE

WISHING FOR NEVERLAND

PART TWO

TRAVELING TO NEVERLAND

PART ONE

Wishing for Neverland

INTRODUCTION

F OR centuries European explorers traveled the face of the
earth in search of lands that did not exist. This book is
about some of those places, to which we have given the
name Neverland.

Why did people believe in such fabulous places? Why,
over the course of hundreds of years, did thousands of them
risk their lives seeking places that never for a moment were
real? And if these places didn't exist, how did people know
about them?

One of the sources of information about Neverland is
the fantastic travel story. Eagerly accepted by listeners and
readers, enormously and lastingly popular, these stories
were often made up by imaginative sailors and had some
basis in fact; many of them were very good indeed. Through
repetition, some of their details began to seem credible. As
a result, people were willing to believe in the existence of
other fantastic places.

Some storytellers defied what we now know of geography. For others, geography itself was an important influence. For example, the choicest geographical fantasies found a home in the mysterious East. Near at hand but inaccessible, vast but untraveled, it quickly became an area where many of the wonders (but not all) were imaginary.

The details of a geographical system exist within a larger framework, often called a world picture. In a literal sense, it is only since the publication of some incredibly beautiful photographs taken by the Apollo astronauts that we have seen a picture of our world. But the term *world picture* implies much more—it is a vision of the earth, of its shape and its place in the universe. It is the ancient Indian vision of a flat disc placed on the back of a gigantic turtle supported by four elephants. And it is the medieval European vision of a sphere at the center of the universe; a sphere within moving spheres of sun, moon, and planets, within a fixed sphere of stars, beyond which lies the Empyrean, the seat of God. A world picture is more what we believe than what we know.

The hazy geography of different world pictures allowed for the existence of many Neverlands in ancient times. Geographical knowledge was severely limited before the time of Columbus, and was matched by an incomplete understanding of natural phenomena. The primary fact about the world before the great age of exploration is not that people believed it was round or flat, but that more of it was unknown than known. An incomplete understanding of geography and of natural phenomena, when coupled with fantastic travel stories, was bound to affect early world pictures.

All this only partly explains Neverland. The willingness of people to believe in nonexistent places was just as important, if not more so. Neverland was the result of an odd state of mind—a worldwide case of "wishing will make it so." We will find as many clues to Neverland in the minds of people as in their maps.

People live in fear of the unknown, but they are also constantly fascinated by it. We pride ourselves on being reasoning creatures, but we often believe things that we know to be unreasonable. The human mind can be terribly clever, and human beings can be terribly foolish. A combination of more fascination than fear, more belief than reason, a large portion of foolishness, and enough cleverness to explain it equals the Neverland state of mind.

CARTA
DELL' AFFRICA
tratta fedelmente dall'Originale

del

Portulano Mediceo Laurenziano

Segnato di N.° 9 Gadd.° Rel.

V. Bandin. Catal.° Bibliot. Leopold. Laurent. T. II. Pag. 11.

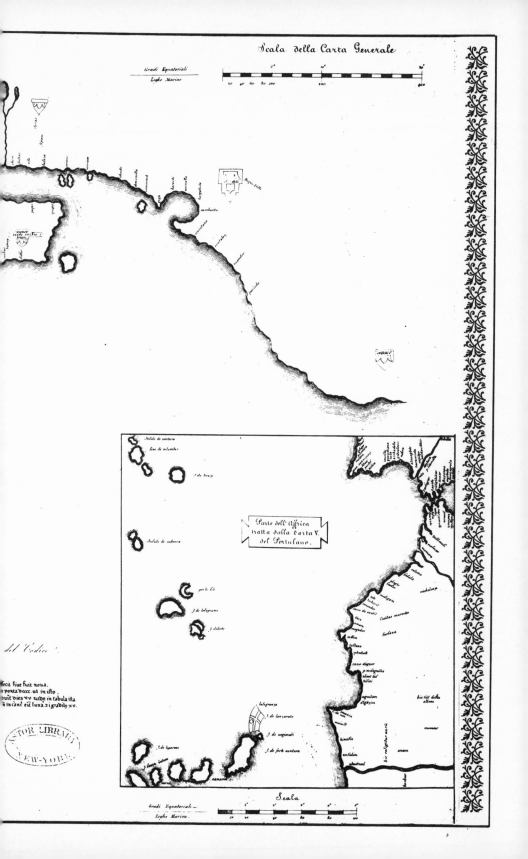

ONE

A Need for Neverland

JUAN Ponce de León was fifty-three years old in 1513. That was a good old age for any man in the early sixteenth century, and especially for an active soldier. He had sailed with Columbus on the Admiral's second voyage, when they discovered Puerto Rico. Afterward Ponce de León conquered the island and was named its governor. He remained an explorer and a tough fighter to the end, killed by Indians in 1521 while trying to kidnap them into slavery.

But in 1513 he must have been feeling his age. He became attracted by a West Indian legend about a miraculous spring somewhere to the north. Bathing in its waters would restore health and vigor to the infirm and youth to the aged. This remarkable Fountain of Youth was supposed to exist on a legendary island named Bimini, probably in the Bahamas. Just drinking from the fountain, some said, would restore one's youth. Whether or not he truly believed in the legend, Ponce de León sailed up from Puerto Rico and cruised through the Bahamas.

In March, 1513, after leaving the Bahamas, he made a significant discovery. It was only a sandy beach with a dense background of tropical greenery. But he had come upon the continental mainland—the first Spanish explorer to reach what is now the United States. Because he first saw this land on Easter Sunday, which the Spaniards then popularly called *Pascua florida* ("flowery Easter"), he called it La Florida.

On April 2, 1513, he landed just north of the present site of St. Augustine, and six days later he took possession of the new land in the name of the Spanish king. Sailing southward, he explored the country's coastline, rounded its cape, and continued up its western shore into the Gulf of Mexico. (Though he demonstrated that the new land was a peninsula, neither he nor his king seem to have noticed.) Returning to Spain in 1514, he was named governor of "The Island of Florida." Seven years later, perhaps still seeking his Fountain of Youth, Ponce de León went back to Florida. He found no magic fountain, only natives who resisted his attempt to enslave them and mortally wounded him.

Why would a practical soldier, conquering explorer, and governor of colonies spend his time, and risk his life searching for a Fountain of Youth? Columbus was at least searching for spices and a shorter sea route to India. Later Spanish, French, and English explorers sought gold, furs, and tobacco. They planted colonies. Why did Ponce de León pursue so unrealistic a quest?

A quest is a search. In some ancient myths and many medieval romances it is also an expedition undertaken by a hero in order to perform some special task. For this reason we tend to associate a quest with an extensive journey. But there are many other kinds of quests—for eternal life, unending happiness, or perfect beauty. We still speak of the quest for power, or for wealth, or for truth. You may be reading this book in a quest for knowledge, or at least for facts.

In Ponce de León's time it was not unrealistic—in fact, it was perfectly reasonable—to believe in a Fountain of Youth. Irish legends had long before told of youth-giving waters off to the west. Although we cannot be sure that Ponce de León knew anything of these legends, they demonstrate that the idea of a Fountain of Youth was widely acceptable. In the sixteenth century belief in the existence of such a geographical wonder was still possible.

Let's look at Ponce de León's quest another way. We can be fairly certain that he would have considered the idea of a spaceship journey to the moon ridiculous. But journeying by land or sea, even in uncharted waters, to no matter what fabulous place, was possible and understandable. Clearly some quests are unreal in one age and even ordinary in another.

In a manner of speaking, Neverland is neither a political nor a geographical state; it is a state of mind. We may scoff at Ponce de León's search for the Fountain of Youth, but in his day it was a quest that was real, whereas journeying to the moon would have been viewed as a trip to Neverland. In the nineteenth century an astronomer described "canals" on Mars. Until very recently even scientifically trained observers discussed their meaning. But now we know from closeup pictures that these "canals" never existed. They were imagined or misinterpreted from insufficient visual evidence. Scientific explanations were as pointless as stories about advanced Martian civilizations. The state of mind that produces a Neverland thrives on incomplete and inaccurate information—often on the nonsense that can fill people's heads in place of knowledge.

Human nature is not always reasonable. We like to hear stories that fill us with wonder or that even actually frighten us. We enjoy being pushed to the edge of our emotions or our beliefs. So it is not surprising that travelers' tales about wonderful adventures in strange and distant lands have been popular for centuries. Fiction or fact, such stories appeal to something deep within us, to a longing for something more mysterious and wonderful than what we have in our everday world.

In these pages, Neverland is simply the name for all those places that people sought and never found, or reached and never recognized; places that never existed (Prester John's kingdom), or were not supposed to exist (Camelot or Atlantis); places that were fancy not fact (El Dorado).

Neverlands are countries of the mind, existing in a geography of the imagination. They have been convenient locations for folk tales or myths, places from which terrible villains or marvelous sorcerers come, and to which magnificent heroes travel. They generally lie "beyond the horizon" or, at the very least, across the sea; are frequently filled with wonders or fabulous treasures; and are usually difficult to reach and seldom visited.

The fantasy lands of literature—fictional places created by imaginative individual authors—are not part of what we have chosen to call Neverland. There is a difference between Oz and El Dorado, for example, or between Middle Earth and the Kingdom of Prester John: One is the literary creation of an imaginative writer; the other is a kind of geographical mass delusion. For this reason we will not be considering some famous imaginary—but literary—journeys: *Gulliver's Travels,* or *Twenty Thousand Leagues Under the Sea,* or Dante's passage through Hell, Purgatory, and Paradise in *The Divine Comedy.*

Not every written account of a fabulous journey is a purely literary creation. Some are folk epics that contain geographical fantasies, or refined and polished versions of frequently-told tales. The voyages of Sinbad the Sailor and St. Brendan are two examples of such tales. At least one epic of adventurous travel, Homer's *Odyssey,* also happens to be a literary masterpiece. But Odysseus is not like Gulliver, nor does he travel to a purely literary creation like Lilliput. Along with Sinbad and Brendan, he voyages through a realm of folk geography.

Readers of *Gulliver's Travels* understand that the events and places have been "made up" by the author. Even sophisticated modern readers accept the fantasies in the *Odyssey* or the story of Sinbad. This is because their adventures read like legends or folk tales, and we assume they are fantasies based on fact. We recognize that some fantastic places were distortions or exaggerations of real places. And we understand that, over the centuries, people truly believed in the reality of places that did not exist.

A number of Neverlands have made it onto the map, or into geography books. Some have appeared on maps for over two centuries even though they never existed for a minute. Some have slipped on due to the misinterpretation of an observation that may have been inaccurate to begin with. Others have made it as a result of hearsay, or were left over from legends. For instance, the "Island of Brazil," or "Brazil Rock," was supposed to be out in the Atlantic, far west of Ireland. It was really a feature carried over from the legends of Atlantis and St. Brendan. Nevertheless, Brazil Rock appeared on British Admiralty charts until 1873.

More than one Neverland, moving from map to map, shifted its location. Some totally imaginary places were actively sought for hundreds of years, and countless people died in the search. On the other hand, it now appears that the most famous Neverland of all, Atlantis, may have actually existed; at least, reputable scientists insist they have found it.

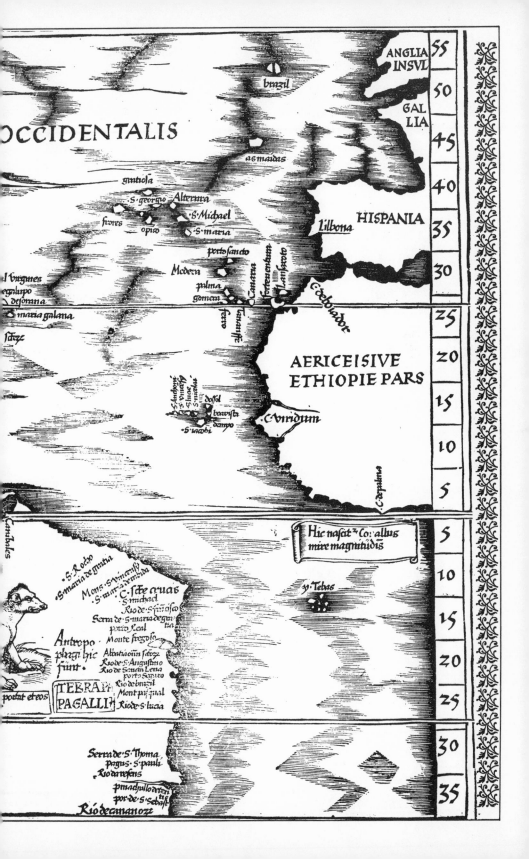

OCCIDENTALIS

ANGLIA INSVL 55

50

GAL LIA 45

40

HISPANIA

l Lilbona 35

30

brazil

asmaidas

gratiosa

S. georgio Alterira

S. Michael

frores opito

S. maria

porto sancto

Medera

fortcuentura

Lançoto

palma Canaria

gomeu

ferro tanarife

C. debiador 25

20

AERICEISIVE
ETHIOPIE PARS

15

S. Anthoni
SS. Vincety
S. Luçie
S. Nicolao

dossol

boavista

dempo

S. Iacobi

C. viridium

10

5

l virgines
e galupo
Desorana

S. maria galana

sctze

Canibales

C. rxpalma

5

Hic naſat͂ ꝫ Co: allus
mire magnitidis

10

y Tebas

15

20

25

S. Rocho

S. maria de gratia

Mons S. Vincenſſ
S. mara aremida

C. ſcte cruas

S. michael

Rio de S. rioſo

Serra de S. maria de grāta

porto real

Monte fregoso

Antropo
phagi hic
ſunt.

Abatiaouū sdorz

Rio de S. Augustino
Rio de Sancta Lena

porto Sanuto

Rio de braſil

Mont priginal

Rio de S. luçia

TERRA
PAGALLI

poſtat et eos

Serra de S. Thoma

pagus. S. paulí

Rio daresens

p̃ma dpullo deſen
por de S. Sebaſt

Rio de camanoze

30

35

Being mysterious or inaccessible is not enough to create a Neverland. For more than two thousand years, the most mysterious place on the face of the earth was the source of the river Nile. Yet it was a real place, and eventually it was found. The South Pole is about as inaccessible as a place can be, but it has been reached several times. Nor does mistaken identity turn a place into a Neverland. On October 12, 1492, one of the most famous voyages of discovery ended when the captain landed at a place other than where he thought he was. But we say Columbus discovered America, not Neverland. The geography of Neverland is not simply mistaken; it is imaginary.

There is a fine distinction between mistaken identity and mistaken belief. When Columbus bumped into a continent (or the outer fringes of two continents), he arrived at a place that, in his mind, shouldn't have been there. But when Captain James Cook discovered Antarctica, he arrived at a place geographers had believed in for twenty centuries. Yet the actual continent, tiny, ice-covered, uninhabited, bore no relation to the Great Unknown Southern Land (*Terra australis incognita*) geographers had expected. Antarctica was real; *Terra australis incognita* was a Neverland.

Although the idea of Neverland satisfies a human longing for mystery, or embodies our fascination with the unknown, many Neverlands have served sound, practical purposes. Though they have both spurred exploration and frightened off explorers, in the main they have helped increase our knowledge of geography. Neverlands have served religion, science, and literature, as we shall see when we come to Prester John, Atlantis, and Camelot. To a surprising extent they have been of great commercial value. More than one Neverland has served to protect a nation's trade, as ancient Phoenician sailors well knew. Some have been of very specific value to individuals or small groups. El Dorado, for example, was worth freedom from prison to Sir Walter Raleigh. Arthurian Britain was politically valuable to the Tudor royal family, and financially rewarding to the monks of Glastonbury. Neverland has often been, literally or figuratively, a gold mine.

Nor can we explain the need to believe in Neverland simply as a quirk of human nature. Practical politics were involved in keeping Camelot or El Dorado alive in the public mind. But political motives have often been influenced by human desires, or gullibility, inaccurate reporting, and a poor sense of geography. We will see later that the mythical realm of Prester John was a comforting idea to cling to when the Asiatic hordes were threatening Europe.

Centuries of tradition suggested that distant places were more powerfully attractive than known lands, even as the known world continued to expand. Aside from religious shrines, one of the most interesting places in the Bible is Tarshish, mainly because it is the most distant. The ancient Greeks spoke often of lands "beyond the horizon." The Romans, when their empire reached its farthest extent, knew there were still mysterious "lands beyond." As long as regions of the world remained unexplored—and even after—Neverland would live.

A poor sense of history or geography, bad reporting and gullible audiences, human failings and human desires, the excitement of mystery and romance—there are many explanations for Neverland. People wanted it to be there, wherever "there" happened to be, for very good reasons. When times were bad, when the real world was harsh, when mountains were too high and seas too wide, when everyday life was boring and travelers told such fanciful stories, who could resist a Fountain of Youth, a lake of gold, or a mountain of gems? Who could deny "facts" that had been part of folk lore for ages? People did not understand that some stories outlive the reasons for telling them. Add to this the books of ancient historians, misleading when written and garbled in a succession of translations, and the result was a world filled with Neverlands.

Travel is not a modern invention. Prehistoric people from Olduvai Gorge moved up through the African continent—a few thousand miles over many thousands of years—into the Cradle of Civilization, Mesopotamia and Egypt. The early centers of civilization, east of the Mediterranean Sea and along its southeastern shore, had their own travelers.

Imagine one of those travelers returning home with the first account of a rhinoceros, or a hippopotamus, or an elephant. What a sensation he must have caused! What did people who were familiar with horses think of the camel when they saw it or had it described to them? It is hardly strange that untraveled people believed in fabulous creatures. How did a traveler from central Europe describe a volcano? How did one from the Mediterranean describe an iceberg? We know that early travel stories tell of mountains of fire and mountains of crystal, and we can almost see the stories "grow" in the telling.

Travelers must have been popular storytellers. They may have begun as reporters, perhaps not very accurate ones either. It is easy enough to move from reporting to embellishing, adding details—perhaps to hold an audience's attention. The next step must have been inventing. A good storyteller had only to make the inventions interesting to hold his audience.

The curious thing is that the stories had to be only moderately convincing, as long as they were fascinating. Distant places held a fascination all their own and human nature did the rest. It made the audiences want to believe in the unconvincing parts. This is no more unusual than our own interest and belief in creatures like the Loch Ness Monster or the Abominable Snowman.

We will be noting a connection between various Neverlands and myths, legends, and folk tales. Myths may be defined as imaginative explanations of natural phenomena; legends, as exaggerated recollections of dimly remembered events; and folk tales as orally repeated popular stories, usually involving a local semihero. The image of the sun as a fiery chariot driven across the sky by a god is an example of a myth. The legendary voyage of the Argonauts, modern scholars tell us, is based on the earliest trading voyages of the Greeks. And many of the adventures of Robin Hood were originally English folk tales.

Myths arose in the absence of scientific explanations. Modern scientists can explain lightning, earthquakes, plagues, even the origin of life. These and other phenomena formed the bases of myths in the ancient world. Folk tales, on the other hand, have nothing to do with such explanations. They survive on their charm, their sense of fun, and their entertainment value. The exploits of Paul Bunyan are folk tales. Some folk heroes, like John Henry or Johnny Appleseed, were real people.

But how do legends arise? There is no simple answer to this question. Most legends have some basis in fact, and it is possible to take them apart and trace their factual beginnings. Each legend, however, has its own set of facts. So each legend can be seen to grow from a different beginning. The key point is that the facts often become distorted in the legend. The original narrator (or narrators) of the legend may have introduced the distortion deliberately, but it is the distortion that gives rise to the legend.

We now know that the dangers faced by some early travelers were purposely exaggerated to frighten off competing travelers. Long ago, the Phoenicians controlled the waters of the Atlantic west of Gibraltar and around the northern bulge of Africa, the seas beyond the Pillars of Hercules. They helped maintain their control by telling hair-raising stories of the dangers that lurked there. Two thousand years after the Phoenicians, these waters still frightened the Portuguese sailors of Prince Henry the Navigator. In the meantime, more than one legend, and more than one Neverland, grew in those waters.

The enduring popularity of travelers' tales, the permanent place of myths, legends, and folk tales in our culture, and the nonexistent places that adorned maps for centuries all have something in common: They are expressions of an eternal human longing to believe in the mysterious.

TWO

Travelers' Tales

THE most familiar group of myths and legends in our culture is that from ancient Greece. It includes two very famous travel stories—the homeward journey of Odysseus after the Trojan War and the voyage of the Argonauts. Both stories contain mythic and legendary material but have a strong basis in fact.

The account of the Argonauts' voyage as we now know it is a combination of material from various sources. The original story is very old. Homer, who presumably lived in the ninth century B.C., said it was familiar to everyone. In other words, by 800 B.C. it was a well established legend. It was written down in detail by Pindar, a Greek poet of the fifth century B.C. And in the third century B.C. Apollonius of Rhodes wrote an epic poem about the voyage, the *Argonautica.* This later version was popular in Roman times. But the original popularity of the story dates from preliterary times, when tales were repeated orally. This complicated background accounts for the variations, inconsistencies, and questions that surround the story.

Set a generation before the Trojan War, it is an account of the first heroic journey of the ancient Greek world. Briefly, it is the story of the hero Jason, who is sent on a dangerous mission to bring back to Greece a treasure known as the Golden Fleece. This treasure hangs in a sacred grove in far off Colchis, where it is guarded by a sleepless dragon.

Jason orders the construction of a fifty-oared vessel for the great journey. It is named *Argo* after its builder, Argos; and the heroes who sail in it become known as the Argonauts. In the various versions of the story almost every available Greek hero has been placed aboard the *Argo*, even though there could have been only fifty of them. Yet certain names remain constant from one version to another. The best known of them include Heracles (Hercules), the greatest of Greek heroes; Orpheus, the famous poet and musician; Peleus, the father of Achilles; the twins, Castor and Polydeuces (Pollux), also familiar to us as the constellation *Gemini*; Argos, the builder of the ship; and a woman, the huntress Atalanta.

The heroes set forth from Greece and are very soon out of familiar waters. Their first stop is Lemnos, an island inhabited only by women. Then they sail past Samothrace and through the Hellespont (the strait separating Europe and Asia) to the island of Cyzicus. The king of Cyzicus receives them hospitably and speeds them on their journey. But a storm at night blows them back and they are mistaken for pirates. In the ensuing battle they unfortunately kill their former host. Following this misadventure Heracles leaves them to search for his armor-bearer, who has been carried off by a water nymph.

In Thrace they rescue a blind seer from the Harpies who are tormenting him. In gratitude he tells Jason how to pass through the Symplegades, two clashing rocks that guard the entrance to the Black Sea. With this advice, and some divine intervention, the *Argo* becomes the first ship to escape the clashing rocks, losing only its rudder in the process. The rocks have remained fixed in place ever since.

Following the southern shore of the Black Sea, the Argonauts pass many strange places and meet with various adventures. Finally they arrive at Colchis, where King Æetes greets them. He agrees to give Jason the prize he has come for—if he proves himself worthy of it. Æetes sets the hero a seemingly impossible task: He must yoke two fierce bulls with bronze feet and flaming breath and make them plow a field; then he must sow dragon's teeth in the furrows he has plowed and fight the armed warriors who crop up instantly from the sown teeth. Jason accepts the challenge without hesitation.

Meanwhile, Æetes' daughter, the enchantress Medea, has fallen in love with Jason. Eros (Cupid), the god of love, struck her with one of his arrows the moment she first saw Jason. Medea provides the hero with an ointment that protects him from the bulls' fiery breath. She also tells him to toss a large rock into the midst of the dragon's-teeth warriors, who battle among themselves and kill each other. With Medea's help Jason succeeds in his impossible task.

Æetes is enraged at this unexpected turn of events and still withholds the Golden Fleece. Once again Medea comes to the rescue. She charms the sleepless dragon guarding the fleece and Jason steals the treasure. When he flees to the *Argo,* she decides she had better go with him. The ship sets sail with Æetes in hot pursuit. Medea's brother is also aboard the *Argo,* which gives her a clever, but unsisterly idea. She kills the boy, cuts his body into pieces, and casts the pieces overboard. Æetes slows his pursuit to pick up the pieces of his son, to reassemble them for proper burial. The *Argo* escapes and heads for home.

Jason subdues the dragon guarding the Golden Fleece, with the help of
Medea's magic potion. In this elaborate seventeenth-century illustration, the fleece hangs over the limb of a tree in the exact center of the
picture.

The different versions of the story provide us with at least four routes for the return journey. Some versions bring the voyagers to Scylla and Charybdis, the rock and whirlpool familiar to readers of Homer's *Odyssey*. They also visit Crete, where Medea overcomes Talos, a man made of bronze. Other routes take them far to the north or south of the main scene of the voyage. The route most frequently cited has the Argonauts sailing up the Danube River and then making their way to the Adriatic Sea. A storm threatens to wreck them off Corfu, northwest of the Greek coast. They are divinely warned that they will not get home unless they visit Circe to be cleansed of the murder of Medea's brother. So they sail by river routes to the Tyrrhenian Sea and Circe's island. They pass the Sirens, and are protected by Orpheus and the magic of his songs; escape the twin perils of Scylla and Charybdis; and then land on the island of the Phaeacians. (These adventures are also familiar elements in the story of Odysseus.)

Another storm that hits when they are near home sends them off course and lengthens their journey. They are blown to Libya—which is often another name for Africa in Greek legends—carry their ship overland to Lake Tritonis, reach the Mediterranean, and sail home by way of Crete. All the versions except the earliest agree that the Argonauts return home across the Mediterranean—that is, from a direction opposite the one in which they originally headed.

So much for the story of the voyage. Jason and Medea move on to another legend. He treats her disgracefully, and she exacts a terrible revenge. This story, told by Euripides in his play *Medea*, is still being performed after two thousand years. Another story tells of an event long after the journey. Jason returns to the *Argo*, which he has set up on dry land as a monument to the voyage. Now an old man, he lies down to rest in the shade of the vessel he commanded so many years before. As he does so, the stern of the ship falls off and kills him. Robert Graves, the well known author and expert on myths, says that the addition of this episode makes Jason's story a moral tale, illustrating the dangers of excessive fame.

Were There Real Argonauts?

More than three thousand years have gone by since Jason's voyage presumably took place; most of the events and the participants in them had become legendary before 500 B.C. How do modern scholars find the facts behind so ancient a legend? In this case there are two principal avenues of research: One is to establish the geography of the story; the other is to find natural phenomena that fit the marvels encountered by the Argonauts. This is not easy at such a distance in time, and is further complicated by the existence of different versions of the Argonaut story.

The earliest versions of the story do not include the fabulous incidents that give it so much color and excitement. And later versions probably incorporate incidents from other voyages, added because they fit nicely into the framework of the basic story. Some details, therefore, can (or must) be dropped as we try to reconstruct the actual voyage that prompted the legend.

The geography of the voyage presents a vexing problem. Much of the geography of the versions dating from the fifth and third centuries B.C. was probably not known at the presumed time of the actual voyage, about 1300 B.C. There are many rivers mentioned in the later versions of the story that turn out to be simply not navigable by a fifty-oared ship. The authors seem to be displaying geographical knowledge unrelated to the story, while skimping on detailed physical descriptions that would help to establish the true geography. This indicates that the story was popular enough to be rewritten centuries later, when its original significance had become obscure.

Even the early versions of the story, however, have Jason set out on his voyage from Orchomenus. We know that Orchomenus was situated in Boeotia, a region about sixty miles northwest of Athens and twenty miles east of Delphi. The only other geographical detail established in the early versions of the story is the island of Lemnos, at the mouth of the Dardanelles. Traveling from Orchomenus to Lemnos at least confirms that the Argonauts were on an eastward voyage.

Fortunately, two guides from ancient times can help us: the the historian Herodotus and the geographer Strabo; but their help is limited. Strabo (c.64 B.C.–A.D. 19), author of the most famous classical compilation of geographical knowledge, tells us that Homer mentioned places around the Black Sea all the way to Colchis. This, of course, covers the route of Jason's voyage. But whatever Homeric references Strabo had in mind, the texts no longer exist for us to examine. Moreover, we know that Colchis was added to the original story by the poet Hesiod, a century after Homer. The best we can say is that the geography of the voyage appears to have been taking shape in Homer's day but was not firmly established even by Herodotus' time, four centuries later.

Herodotus (c.484–c.424 B.C.), as we shall see throughout this book, is a fascinating source of information about the ancient world. From him we learn that both a city and a river in Colchis were named Phasis. He says that Greeks who traveled to Phasis found there an unusual bird with brilliant plumage that had a most pleasant flavor when cooked. The bird was called *phasianos*, after its place of origin, and the name is carried down into modern English

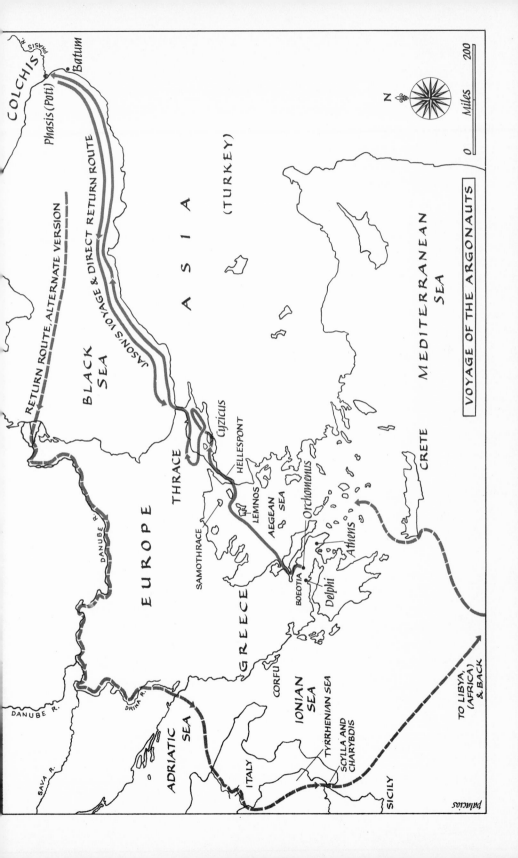

PHASIS R.

COLCHIS

Batum

Phasis (Poti)

BLACK SEA

RETURN ROUTE, ALTERNATE VERSION

JASON'S VOYAGE & DIRECT RETURN ROUTE

ASIA

(TURKEY)

N

200
Miles
0

MEDITERRANEAN SEA

EUROPE

THRACE

Cyzicus

HELLESPONT

LEMNOS

SAMOTHRACE

AEGEAN SEA

Orchomenus

GREECE

BOEOTIA

Delphi

Athens

CRETE

DANUBE R.

DANUBE R.

SAVA R.

DRINA R.

ADRIATIC SEA

CORFU

IONIAN SEA

ITALY

TYRRHENIAN SEA

SCYLLA AND CHARYBDIS

SICILY

TO LIBYA, (AFRICA) & BACK

VOYAGE OF THE ARGONAUTS

palacios

as pheasant. Today we identify Colchis as Georgia, in southern Russia. The river called Phasis is the Rion, in the Caucasus. The city of Phasis is Poti, an oil city north of Batum. This last identification is based on information from Herodotus, who describes Phasis as a city built on wooden piles in an iridescent swamp; it was the area's main export center for pitch.

When we get to the return journey we find ourselves faced with a summary of practically all the fact and fancy of classical Greek geography. This is because the different versions of the story describe a variety of routes, all of them complicated. Pindar's route presumably runs from the Black Sea to the Indian Ocean, via the Caspian and Aral seas and the Oxus and Indus rivers, across Libya for twelve days to Lake Tritonis. The details are not clear, but the inclusion of Lake Tritonis is most interesting. It may even have been put in simply *because* it was so interesting. Lake Tritonis was once an enormous inland sea in northern Africa. Since very ancient times, however, it has been shrinking, and is now nothing but salt marshes. In classical times, according to existing records, it was about nine hundred square miles in area.

From different versions of the story, modern scholars can work out in detail at least three other routes. One takes the heroes up the Danube River, into the heart of Europe, to the Rhine, and by other rivers back to the Mediterranean. The strangest route takes them up the Don and Volga rivers to the Arctic Ocean, from there through the Baltic Sea or around Norway, and home through the Pillars of Hercules. This route, which circumnavigates Europe, must date from classical Greek times, when the Don was thought to have its source in the Gulf of Finland. Some scholars suggest that the heroes reached northwest Europe by carrying their boat from river to river, and that they sailed around Ireland and past Spain into the Mediterranean.

The simplest and most logical route for the return journey would have been for the heroes to come back the way they went, through the Hellespont. Early versions of the story seem to imply that they did. Why then did later versions ignore this simple route? It is thought that Jason's complicated return journeys are folk memories of lost trade routes from the remote past. In other words, real traders of Jason's time followed routes that were dimly recalled when the Argonaut story was retold many centuries later. Archaeologists have reconstructed an ancient trade route similar to Jason's return voyage by way of the Danube, though it does not extend as far west as the Rhine. Instead, it runs from the Danube to the Semmering Pass in the Alps southwest of present day Vienna, into what is now Yugoslavia, across the Sava River and the Nanos Mountains, and down to the Mediterranean.

Some of the hazards Jason faced can also be connected to trade routes. Not all the details in the story are fanciful descriptions of natural phenomena. Some of them can be given bases in fact; others must be considered symbolic; and a few are literary devices, borrowed from other legends. The clashing rocks have been explained as ice floes from Russian rivers adrift in the Black Sea. On the other hand, such rocks are mentioned in the *Odyssey* and may have been "moved" east simply for the sake of the story. Herodotus indicates that Phasis was situated in the midst of oil fields. This suggests that the fire-breathing bulls may be symbols of plowing amid smoke and flame, or in the middle of an area of burning oil.

The object most in need of explanation is the Golden Fleece, presumably a late addition to the story. This heavily guarded, magic-enshrouded treasure has a secretive and mysterious air about it that suggests a carefully protected trade route. Colchis was the end of the Asian caravan routes. Excavations there have uncovered ancient treasures from the Orient, possibly China, a trade connection that would have made Colchis exceedingly attractive to bold voyagers from Greece. Trade routes by sea from Greece to Colchis were probably established about 1300 B.C., or roughly the time of the story; thus the legend is undoubtedly based on an actual voyage or voyages that took place before the Trojan War. The voyages are most likely concerned with trade, though possibly with piracy. In this light, the fabled fleece either represents actual gold or is symbolic of the riches of the Orient.

Over the years scholars have offered numerous interesting explanations of the Golden Fleece, but the most common is the one first provided by Strabo in his *Geographica*, two thousand years ago. He reports that the natives of Colchis placed hides or sheepskins in the swift-running Phasis River to catch particles of gold washed down from the mountains. This naturalistic explanation of the Golden Fleece is widely accepted because it is both simple and reasonable. However, many scholars prefer to see the Golden Fleece as a symbolic, rather than a real, object.

Attempting to explain all the features of a legend, particularly this one, leads to contradictions and confusion. Part of the geographical confusion surrounding the story, says Robert Graves, comes from the inclusion of both Colchis and Circe's island. This island lies off the west coast of Italy, and Colchis is fifteen hundred miles to the east. The story says the Argonauts got from one to the other by river routes. But Graves points out that some rivers along the presumed route would not have been navigable by a ship of the *Argo*'s size. For this reason, he says, other versions of the story introduced the Lake Tritonis route. He suggests moving the story from the Black Sea to the Adriatic.

This suggestion is at odds with the earliest versions of the story, which clearly indicate a voyage to the east. But it offers an answer to a basic and puzzling question. Why, in the later versions, do the Argonauts always return from a westerly direction? The story remains fascinating despite such puzzles, because it is such a good narrative. And it can be said for all Neverlands that explaining their mysteries does not diminish their fascination.

The Wanderings of Odysseus

The story of Odysseus' homeward journey comes to us from a single source, Homer's *Odyssey,* an epic poem that is one of the earliest masterworks of western literature. It has remained popular for well over twenty-five hundred years. After it was first composed it was memorized and recited for centuries, and still is in Greece. And it has been printed and reprinted countless times in dozens of languages. It is not only the greatest travel story to come down to us from ancient Greece, it is one of the best adventure stories of all time.

This enduring epic poem was probably created in the ninth century B.C., and was possibly even written down at that early date. It tells of events that took place in the early twelfth century B.C. More than three thousand years later, scholars are still studying the poem and "identifying" places described in it. The real appeal of the *Odyssey,* however, lies in the story it has to tell.

The central theme of the *Odyssey* concerns the wanderings and adventures of Odysseus after the Trojan War. Odysseus spent ten years fighting at Troy; according to some legends he was the Greek general who devised the famous Trojan Horse used to conquer the city. As the *Odyssey* tells us, it takes him another ten years to return home to Ithaca. The events of the poem cover only a little more than a month at the end of this ten-year period; in fact, Odysseus himself tells the story of his wanderings during the course of one night. Thus the most familiar material of the epic, what we consider its theme, occupies only a small portion of the whole work. Nevertheless, that material is so vivid that we have come to call any extended adventurous journey an odyssey.

Following the destruction of Troy, Odysseus and about six hundred Ithacans sail for home in twelve ships. They stop first for a raid on Thrace, but then head south. Near the southern tip of the Peloponnesus a storm drives them farther south to the land of the lotus-eaters. Some of Odysseus' men eat the lotus, the fruit of forgetfulness, and have to be carried back to their ships. Next the travelers come to the land of the Cyclopes, barbaric one-eyed giants who live in caves.

Odysseus and twelve of his men are trapped in the cave of a Cyclops named Polyphemus when he returns with his flocks and shuts the mouth of the cave with a huge rock. Polyphemus kills and eats two of Odysseus' men. The next day, in the giant's absence, Odysseus and his remaining men sharpen a large stake. When Polyphemus returns to the cave Odysseus brings out a wineskin he has carried with him. Chatting with the Cyclops and telling him that his name is "Nobody," Odysseus gets Polyphemus drunk. While the giant sleeps in a drunken stupor, Odysseus and his men heat the pointed stake in a fire and drive it into the monster's single eye.

Polyphemus, in agony, roars for help, but the other Cyclopes ignore him when he says "Nobody" has attacked him. At dawn, when Polyphemus releases his flocks, the Ithacans escape by clinging to the undersides of the sheep. The blind Cyclops cannot see them; nor does he feel them when touching the backs of his departing sheep. Back aboard his ship Odysseus cannot resist taunting Polyphemus; and he also tells him his real name. Polyphemus hurls a boulder at the departing ships and prays to his father, Poseidon, the sea god, to avenge him by keeping Odysseus from reaching his home.

Next the travelers reach the island of Aeolus, the god of the winds. Aeolus gives Odysseus a bag that holds all the winds except the one necessary to blow his ships home. Odysseus' men, thinking he is withholding a treasure from them, open the bag just as they come in sight of Ithaca. The winds rush out and blow the ships far off their course, and Odysseus and his men wind up in the land of the Laestrygonians. These giant cannibals devour everyone but Odysseus and the crew of his own ship. The remaining ship then sails to Aeaea, the island home of Circe, a goddess and enchantress.

Odysseus sends half his men to explore the island. Circe welcomes them, but then drugs them and turns them into swine. Odysseus, protected by a magic herb provided by the god Hermes (Mercury), overpowers Circe and makes her restore his men to human form. Even without magic, Circe is enchanting enough for Odysseus to remain with her a year. When he finally decides to leave, Circe tells him he must visit Hades to consult the prophet Teiresias about his future. Circe provides instructions for the voyage to the end of the world, where lies the entrance to Hades, the abode of the dead, the underworld.

In Hades Odysseus meets numerous spirits of the dead. The first is the ghost of Elpenor, the youngest member of his crew, who died accidentally just before they sailed and remains unburied on Circe's island. He is followed by the spirits of many famous men and women, including Teiresias, who foretells Odysseus' future. After leaving Hades, Odysseus returns to Circe's island to bury Elpenor. Before his final departure, Circe advises him about how to meet some of the hazards he will face.

The first hazard is the Sirens, sea nymphs whose beautiful and seductive singing lures sailors into shipwreck. Odysseus listens to their song by having himself strapped to the mast of his ship while his men stop up their ears with wax. The next hazard is to pass through the dangerous narrow strait between two monsters, Scylla and Charybdis. They manage this, but lose six men. Finally they come to the island where the sacred cattle of the sun are kept. Odysseus warns his men not to harm the cattle, but they are becalmed on the island so long they use up their provisions and finally slay and eat some of the sacred animals.

When, at last, they leave the island, Zeus destroys their ship with a thunderbolt as a punishment for eating the sacred cattle. Odysseus alone survives, and reaches the island of Ogygia, home of the nymph Calypso. There he is forced to remain for seven years because of Poseidon's anger at him for blinding Polyphemus.

The Sirens attempt to lure Odysseus, who is tied to the mast of his ship. Because their ears are stuffed with wax, his sailors cannot hear the Sirens' alluring but deadly song.

While Poseidon is busy elsewhere, the other gods tell Calypso to release the unhappy wanderer. She sends him off to Ithaca on a raft. After seventeen days at sea, and within sight of home, Odysseus is spotted by Poseidon, who angrily rouses up a storm that wrecks the raft. Helped by a sea goddess, Ino, Odysseus swims for two days and arrives exhausted on the island of Scheria, home of the Phaeacians. He is welcomed by King Alcinous and becomes a guest at the Phaeacian court. There, one evening, he tells the story of his three years of adventure and wandering, from the fall of Troy to his shipwreck on Calypso's Island. The next morning a Phaeacian ship takes him to Ithaca, and after a day's journey he is finally back in his homeland. Though half of Homer's poem remains, and Odysseus' adventures are not over, his wanderings have come to an end.

Tracing Odysseus' Route

Whether or not a real Odysseus made a real voyage in the twelfth century B.C., the geography of Homer's poem has fascinated scholars and explorers for centuries. They have placed the events of the *Odyssey* in a wide area ranging from the Black Sea to the Atlantic Ocean. Before we join in this geographical free-for-all we should keep in mind a few basic points. In all likelihood, Homer had a direct knowledge of the Aegean area, but of little else, at least at firsthand. It is also likely that, through the Phoenicians, Greeks of Homer's day did know something of a wider area. It is possible that the poet had some reasonably good knowledge of an area north to Thrace, south to Egypt, and west to Sicily and southern Italy. We have already noted that Homer may or may not have known of Colchis, to the east, but he probably had some knowledge of the Black Sea. There is no evidence that Greeks of the ninth century B.C.

had a clear geographic understanding of anything beyond these limits.

The earliest known Greek map of the world dates from the sixth century B.C. By this time Greek "experts" were offering their interpretations of the geography of the *Odyssey*. Unfortunately, they succeeded only in making things complicated for all future interpreters of the voyage.

Most reconstructions of Odysseus' wanderings stay within the confines of the Mediterranean, and most of the events do seem to have taken place in and around that sea. The number of places identified by interpreters of Homer suggest that there is more than just poetry or legend attached to the voyage. However, even assuming some factual basis to the story, we must allow for one other assumption. It is quite possible that Odysseus' wanderings represent the combined travels of many ancient sailors.

There has been, over the years, a surprising amount of agreement about a number of the identifications. The land of the lotus-eaters is generally thought to be that part of the North African coast between the Gulf of Sidra in Libya and the Gulf of Gabes in Tunisia. Some ancient scholars located it more specifically at Djerba, an island in the Gulf of Gabes. The lotus itself has often been explained as a poppy. The poppy is a source of opium, which would produce the forgetfulness described in the story. But modern scholars think the lotus is more probably the jujube, a datelike sweet fruit still grown in the area.

According to ancient tradition, the island of the Cyclopes is Sicily. The Roman poet Virgil said that angry Polyphemus was the personification of Mt. Aetna, a volcano on that island. The Cyclops' one big eye is the volcano's crater; the mountain top or boulder he hurls at Odysseus is descriptive of a volcanic eruption. The numerous caves that exist throughout Sicily have been noted as confirmation of this traditional identification.

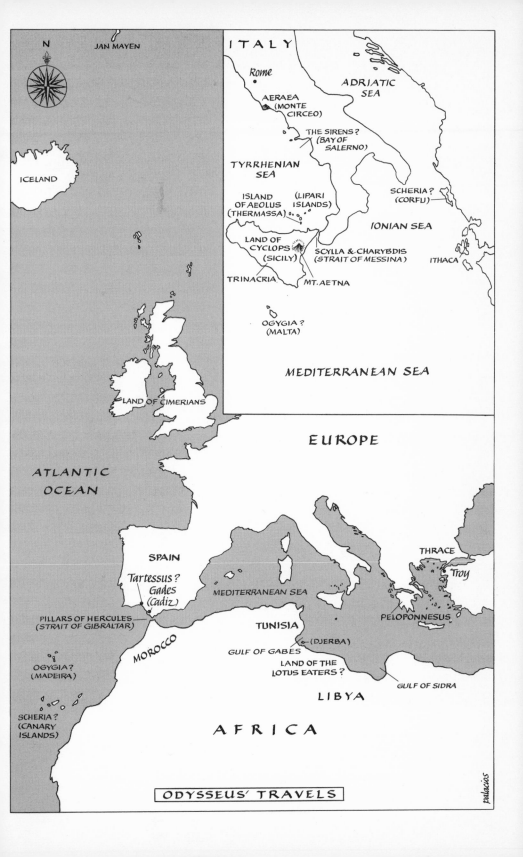

N

JAN MAYEN

ICELAND

ITALY

Rome

AERAEA
(MONTE
CIRCEO)

THE SIRENS?
(BAY OF
SALERNO)

**ADRIATIC
SEA**

TYRRHENIAN
SEA

ISLAND
OF AEOLUS
(THERMASSA)

(LIPARI
ISLANDS)

SCHERIA?
(CORFU)

IONIAN SEA

LAND OF
CYCLOPS
(SICILY)

SCYLLA & CHARYBDIS
(STRAIT OF MESSINA)

ITHACA

TRINACRIA

MT. AETNA

OGYGIA?
(MALTA)

MEDITERRANEAN SEA

LAND OF CIMERIANS

EUROPE

**ATLANTIC
OCEAN**

THRACE

Troy

SPAIN

Tartessus?
Gades
(Cadiz)

MEDITERRANEAN SEA

PELOPONNESUS

PILLARS OF HERCULES
(STRAIT OF GIBRALTAR)

TUNISIA

(DJERBA)

MOROCCO

GULF OF GABES

LAND OF THE
LOTUS EATERS?

OGYGIA?
(MADEIRA)

GULF OF SIDRA

LIBYA

SCHERIA?
(CANARY
ISLANDS)

AFRICA

palacios

ODYSSEUS' TRAVELS

A different explanation of the Cyclops was offered in the fourteenth century by the famous Italian author Giovanni Boccaccio. He said that the remains of Polyphemus had been found in a Sicilian cave, and that they indicated the monster had been a three-hundred-foot giant. Athanasius Kircher, examining Polyphemus' bones three hundred years later, said they showed him to have been only thirty feet tall. Actually, what both men examined were the bones of an elephant. And what both of them took to be the single eye socket of the Cyclops was the trunk opening in the elephant's skull.

Another ancient and traditional identification concerns the island of Aeolus, the god of the winds. It is usually placed in the Lipari Islands, off the west coast of southern Italy. One of these islands, Thermassa, had a distinctive feature in ancient times—a volcano with a constant smoke plume rising from it. The shifting plume of smoke was used by sailors to find the direction of the wind. This useful and well-known natural wonder provides a logical link between Thermassa (now called Vulcano) and the island of Aeolus.

Not all the places in the story can be located so conveniently. The description of the land of the Laestrygonians has been said to fit more than a dozen places, as far west as Leontini, in Sicily, and as far east as Balaklava, in the Crimea. There is an unclear and rather confusing reference in the poem to "the nearness of night and day." This has naturally suggested some place in the far north, a place distant from the Mediterranean Sea. As early as 170 B.C. the land of the Laestrygonians was being identified with Thule, the northernmost point of the classical world. But this interpretation of a confusing reference in the poem does not jibe with the presumed course of Odysseus' wanderings. Some modern scholars suggest that the reference simply concerns the tending of different flocks in the night and in the day.

There are no detailed clues to the identity of Aeaea, Circe's island. It has been thought to be Monte Circeo, on the Italian coast south of Rome, which looks like an island when viewed from the sea. On the other hand, it has also frequently been identified as Malta. Placing it on the west coast of Italy, however, locates it more conveniently for Odysseus' trip to the underworld.

The entrance to Hades is almost always assumed to be far to the west. Homer's description of it is as clouded over with confusing references as the place itself is covered with eternal fog and "darkness of mist and of cloud." To some interpreters these references suggest the coast of Morocco, which is covered by dense fog much of the year. To others they suggest the Atlantic Ocean, which is much more overcast than the Mediterranean Sea. The general location is supposed to be in the "land of the Cimmerians." This land, according to Homer, lay at the limits of the world, in the stream Oceanus. It is pictured as being shrouded in mist and clouds, a land where the sun never shines.

Herodotus offers no help in this matter. He identifies an actual group of people as Cimmerians, but places them to the north of the Black Sea. Modern scholarship, however, has introduced a fascinating explanation for the Cimmerians. It has been noted that a Celtic tribe in Britain, producers of tin in ancient times, called themselves Cymry. Here is an association with both the name Cimmerian and the far-western entrance to the underworld.

There are other clues which suggest that Odysseus wandered out into the Atlantic. But the traditional view is that his voyages took him around the Mediterranean. For example, a long-standing tradition has associated the Sirens with three rocks off the Italian coast, in the Bay of Salerno. The traditional location of Scylla and Charybdis is also in the Mediterranean. Although this identification dates from ancient times, it has remained in dispute. Clearly, from the description in Homer, Charybdis is a whirlpool. This limits possible sites to some extent. The dangerous passage between the two monsters is traditionally said to be the Strait of Messina, between Italy and Sicily; the whirlpool off Sicily said to be personified as Charybdis was well known to classical writers.

As far back as Strabo, however, we find the suggestion that the passage in question was really the Strait of Gibraltar. (Strabo, you recall, is the Greek geographer who guided us to some of the places in the voyage of the Argonauts.) The validity of his theory depends upon how we explain the other monster, Scylla. This horrible monster is described as having a dozen feet and six long, curving necks. Perhaps this is an imaginative description of a giant octopus, which holds itself in place with two legs and reaches out for any passing prey with its other six. Giant octopi do occur near Gibraltar, and the naturalist Pliny wrote of one in Roman times. Presumably it was a strange and frightening beast in Homer's time. At any rate, it was not then part of the Greek diet as it is today.

Did Odysseus sail out into the Atlantic? The traditional view opposes this theory, but convincing arguments have been put forward to support it. For example, consider Thrinacia, the island of the sacred cattle of the sun. It is traditionally identified with Sicily, an island called *Trinacria* in Latin, because of its triangular shape. But, if Odysseus was sailing west from Gibraltar when he reached Thrinacia, the traditional identification does not hold up. Quite to the contrary, he would have to wind up somewhere in the Atlantic.

The case of Ogygia, Calypso's island, serves the Atlantic argument even better. Several descriptions of Ogygia appear in the *Odyssey*. It is a heavily wooded, subtropical island, situated at "the navel of the ocean." These descriptions do not fit Malta, in the Mediterranean, which is traditionally suggested as Ogygia, although the island of Malta, again by tradition, was often called the navel of the ocean. The descriptions do fit Madeira, however, an island out in the Atlantic. In addition, astronomical and geographical calculations based on the account of Odysseus' voyage from Ogygia seem to confirm that the island is really Madeira.

Modern scholars have grown more convinced that Homer's *Odyssey*, knowingly or unknowingly, reflects some knowledge of the Atlantic. One recent interpreter has placed Odysseus as far from Greece as Iceland. Other distant places have appealed over the centuries to the many people who have tried to reconstruct Odysseus' wanderings. If agreement about the location of some sites is surprisingly wide, there is amazing disagreement about the location of other sites; for example, the Phaeacians of Scheria have been located as far east as the Arabian Sea and as far west as the Canary Islands.

Obviously, a great many questions arise in trying to reconstruct Odysseus' wanderings. Some of them will probably never be answered to everyone's satisfaction. But it seems clear enough that much of Odysseus' voyage can be traced. Some of it can be guessed at with reasonable certainty. Adventurous modern sailors have covered the presumed course of the voyage in small vessels. Their trips have added to the long-standing belief that the voyage was not a fictitious one, even though no trace of Odysseus has ever been found.

Sinbad the Sailor

Early fantastic travel stories, like those about Jason and Odysseus, were primarily tales of adventure. Later ones, even later versions of the Argonaut story, had fabulous background details that began to "compete" with the adventure itself.

By medieval times, as familiar stories were repeated and new ones came into circulation, some of the more colorful details became detached from their original sources, as if they were too good to limit to one hero or one story. A number of fabulous incidents and descriptions began to appear in various stories from around the world. For example, the whale that is mistaken for an island appears several times in this book.

We know now that the voyages of Jason and Odysseus were specific voyages, and that the details of those journeys applied to specific places. There are, as we have seen, good, solid reasons to place Jason in the Black Sea and Odysseus in the Mediterranean. But when we come to Sinbad the Sailor we are faced with something else. It is at least two thousand years later, and a general collection of tall tales of the sea has grown up, gathered from all over the known world. These fanciful episodes have no specific geographic attachments. They are separate little goodies, perfect for throwing into a story one or two at a time, like spices in a stew.

Such a collection of incidents and stories could, and did, exist independently, and a clever storyteller could invent a hero or a voyage around which to weave a selection of such tall tales: Sinbad the Sailor fits the bill nicely. The tall tales of the sea were already well established; Sinbad, hardly larger than life, or even a folk hero, is just a character in a series of related stories.

Along with Aladdin, Ali Baba, and Scheherezade, Sinbad the Sailor is one of the most familiar figures from *The Arabian Nights.* The story of his seven voyages is one of the best known of the tales in that remarkable collection, which reached its present form in the middle of the fifteenth century. He is undoubtedly a wholly fictitious creation. Some scholars, attempting to seek the origins of the story, note that the Arabic name for India is "Sind," and that Sinbad's adventures take place in the Indian Ocean. But Sinbad's origins, and even his "identity," are unimportant.

It is the familiarity of Sinbad's adventures that seems to have kept them alive and popular. Although they are, in part at least, a grab bag of old sailors' tales of the sea, some of the incidents are clearly related to episodes in much older stories, such as the *Odyssey*. Others appear in completely unrelated stories, whose settings are far distant from the Indian Ocean.

However, if we examine the story of Sinbad, we find there is also some relation in it to actual facts and places. A map can be charted for his voyages, although it is less clear than the one we can construct for Odysseus or Jason. And the factual touches in the story remind us that Sinbad's seven voyages take place in an ocean that was quite familiar to Arab traders of the medieval world. In the story, however, it becomes an ocean more fanciful than factual.

On his first voyage, becalmed in the Indian Ocean, Sinbad and some companions climb onto what they think is an island. Actually, it is a sleeping whale. They light a fire and awaken the whale, who dives underwater. Sinbad, whose luck always holds after initial misfortune, is eventually picked up and returns home.

On his second voyage Sinbad is left on an island where he discovers an enormous roc's egg. The roc is a fantastically huge bird, and Sinbad fastens himself to one of its claws. Carried to a valley of diamonds by the roc, Sinbad is rescued by diamond-hunting merchants. On his third voyage he meets with another oversized, but more familiar creature, the Cyclops. His fourth voyage takes him to a strange island where he marries a rich lady. When his wife dies, Sinbad is buried alive along with her, according to the local custom. They are interred in a catacomb, from which Sinbad manages to escape. He returns to Baghdad loaded down with valuables taken from the many bodies buried in the catacomb. It must be said that Sinbad is certainly able to make the most of his opportunities.

Two rocs figure in Sinbad's fifth voyage. They destroy his ship by dropping enormous stones on it. Displaying his

Sinbad uses his turban to tie himself to the foot of a giant roc.

great talent for being a sole survivor, Sinbad swims to a desert island. He survives at first by resorting to a delightful trick. He throws rocks at monkeys in the trees and they throw back coconuts which are growing beyond his reach. On the island he later meets the Old Man of the Sea. This strange character climbs on Sinbad's back and remains fastened there for many days and nights. Greatly distressed, not to say uncomfortable, Sinbad finally gets his tormentor drunk and kills him.

The most familiar episodes in the story occur in these first five voyages. Sinbad's sixth voyage takes him to the island of Serendip, which we know to be Ceylon. There he climbs the mountain where Adam went to live when he was expelled from Paradise. On his seventh voyage Sinbad is attacked by pirates and sold into slavery. He is made to shoot elephants so that his master can obtain the valuable tusks. When he tells his master of a hill he has found that is covered with elephants' tusks he is set free and returns home.

That, briefly, is Sinbad's story, without most of the fantastic and fascinating details that make it so entertaining. The details, as we have noted, come largely from a worldwide reservoir of nautical legends and travelers' tales. However, some of the Sinbad episodes appear in other stories. For example, on his sixth voyage Sinbad arrives at Serendip by journeying on a river that runs through a mountain. A remarkably similar journey is taken by Duke Ernest and his companion Wetzel, in a twelfth-century German romance. The whale that is mistaken for an island—a familiar item in medieval sea tales—figures in the story of St. Brendan, and was entertaining Irish audiences as early as the eighth century.

By the time the Sinbad story was written the colorful background details had clearly begun to compete with the adventure story. There existed a number of books on geography and natural history that were crammed with such details, and some of them were very popular.

In the case of the Sinbad story we can determine with great accuracy the origin of many of the details. The incident of the whale is so popular that it may seem too widespread to trace. Nevertheless, we find it in *Wonders of Animate Creation,* a work on natural history dating from about 1280, written by the Arab scholar Qazwini. The wording is strikingly similar to that used in the Sinbad story. In fact, Qazwini and a twelfth-century Arab geographer, Idrisi, are the chief sources of the Sinbad material. The rescue by a giant bird (though not a roc), is another incident that can be traced to Qazwini. An interesting detail from Sinbad's second voyage, the eagles that gather diamonds, also comes from Qazwini's natural history book, and appears in Marco Polo's account of his travels. Such details of natural history had a way of reappearing, sometimes in slightly altered form, throughout ancient and medieval times.

The most unusual creature in the Sinbad story is surely the giant bird, the roc. The story, in keeping with the legends of the time, places its home far beyond the horizon. Marco Polo, however, placed it in Madagascar, where he said it arrived in certain seasons from somewhere far to the south. The Great Khan, according to Marco Polo, sent envoys to Madagascar who returned to China with an enormous feather from a roc. What it was the envoys brought back is not known for sure. Some scholars believe it was a palm frond. Madagascar, however, does have something to offer for our consideration. The elephant bird, *Aepyornis ungens,* a flightless bird like the emu or ostrich, was found there as late as the mid-seventeenth century. Though not as big as the roc in Sinbad's story, it nevertheless laid the biggest eggs ever reported. They were six times the size of

Sinbad overcomes the Old Man of the Sea. The nineteenth-century artist seems to have subscribed to the modern theory that relates the creature to an orangutan.

an ostrich egg, or a hundred and fifty times the size of a chicken egg. If such a bird could fly—well, that's what good storytellers are for.

Natural references, odd and otherwise, help set the geography of Sinbad's voyages. Details in the story of his first voyage are thought to refer to Borneo. Actually, medieval Arab geographers thought India was composed of islands, and they considered Borneo the farthest of these islands. Sinbad's rescuers in his second voyage set him ashore on an island inhabited by the rhinoceros, presumably, either Sumatra or Java. References in the story of his fourth voyage also suggest Sumatra. (Borneo, Java and Sumatra all border the eastern reaches of the Indian Ocean.) Also on his fourth voyage—before he comes to the kingdom where he marries—Sinbad escapes from cannibals. This incident is straight out of Qazwini, who places them on an island called Saksar. Scholars have said this island is either Sumatra or Zanzibar. One glance at a map, however, shows us that Sumatra and Zanzibar are at opposite sides of the Indian Ocean.

How one fixes the geography of the voyages depends upon how one interprets the clues. The "Old Man of the Sea" is generally understood to refer to an orangutan, because the word *orangutan* in Malay means "forest man," and the ape was regarded as a wild human by the earliest western observers. This interpretation places the fifth voyage in Sumatra or Borneo. It has been pointed out however, that the translation name "Old Man of the Sea" is more romantic than accurate: A closer translation that has been offered is "Chief of the Shore," which would seem to suit the orangutan a little better.

Sinbad's third voyage brings in the Cyclops, and the story is clearly related to that of Odysseus and Polyphemus. The Cyclops, as we know, is traditionally associated with

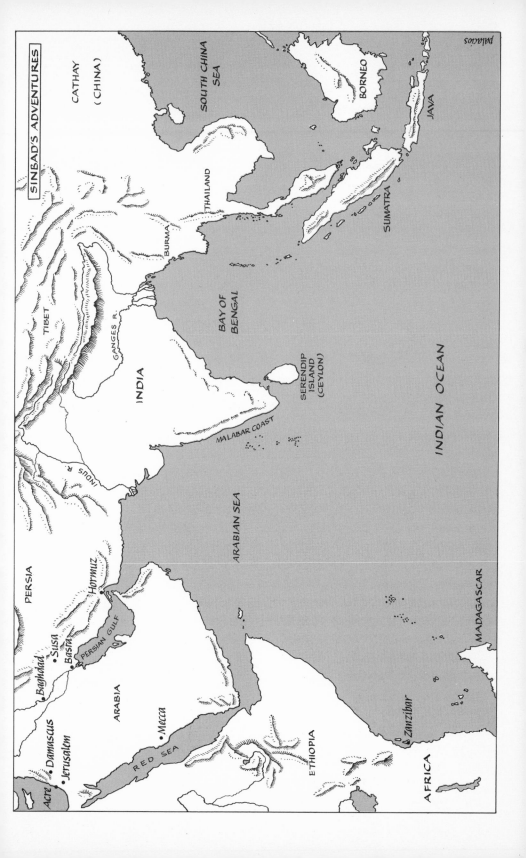

Sicily, a Mediterranean island that was familiar territory to the Arabs of the Middle Ages. The monster has obviously been "moved" far to the east for storytelling purposes—but where? Escaping from the Cyclops, Sinbad meets a huge serpent and comes to an island abounding in sandalwood. To authors L. Sprague de Camp and Willy Ley these clues suggest an island near Java. They believe the man-eating serpent is based upon the Komodo monitor, the so-called dragon of Komodo, a twenty-foot lizard which is a frightening creature even to modern scientific observers.

Research into the Sinbad story has been hampered by the way *The Arabian Nights* has come down to us. *The Thousand and One Nights,* to give it its proper title, was first translated for western readers by a Frenchman, Antoine Galland. His version, published in French in twelve volumes, appeared over a period of several years starting in 1704. Later translations into other western languages were usually made from Galland's, even though his version was more of a paraphrase than an accurate translation. The most famous English translation, by Sir Richard Burton in the nineteenth century, was done from an Egyptian source. So most readers know Sinbad only at second or third hand. From all the evidence, furthermore, it seems likely that the collection of tales familiar to us as *The Arabian Nights* evolved over a period of centuries. If so, this makes it all the more likely that Sinbad's voyages are probably a wonderful grab bag of popular sea legends and travelers' tales. But what a wonderful grab bag!

Brendan the Navigator

The tales associated with one particular traveler lead us to a specific Neverland. That traveler is a sixth-century Irish saint named Brendan, and the nonexistent island, or group of islands, named for him is one of the geographical oddities of the Middle Ages. St. Brendan's Isle, located somewhere in the Atlantic Ocean, appeared on maps in the thirteenth century and remained for hundreds of years. It lingered in Atlantic sea lore until the early eighteenth century, when it was finally explained away as a mirage. But St. Brendan's Isle (or Isles) was no mirage. It was a genuine Neverland.

Medieval geographers filled the Atlantic with mythical islands. The historian Samuel Eliot Morison has noted that sailors called them "Flyaway Islands," because wherever they were supposed to be, they weren't there when anyone reached that location. Brazil Rock, mentioned in Chapter One, was one of these "Flyaway Islands." One of the largest, at least on medieval maps, was Antilia, the Isle of the Seven Cities. So strong was the belief in Antilia, and so persistent, that the West Indies are known to this day as the Antilles.

Even though St. Brendan's Isle didn't exist, it played a role in the great age of discovery. Starting about 1420, Portugal's Prince Henry the Navigator sent his sea captains out on voyages of exploration. By the end of the century they had sailed far out into the Atlantic, rounded Africa, reached India, and established an overseas empire. In 1431, while examining his collection of old maps, Prince Henry noticed the Isles of St. Brendan, apparently a few hundred miles off the Strait of Gibraltar. He sent one of his captains out to locate them. Of course, the captain couldn't find them, but he did discover the Azores. The discovery of these islands, about a thousand miles west of Portugal, excited great interest in further voyages of exploration. At the same time, the discovery strengthened the belief that the Atlantic Ocean was dotted with islands.

But what about the saint himself? He is the central figure in one of the best travel tales of the Middle Ages.

More than one legend grew up around him, and these legends were what put his island on the map.

There was an actual St. Brendan, who lived in the sixth century and sailed the seas around Ireland. Since the ninth century, however, there has also been a strictly legendary St. Brendan. The legendary Brendan may be a colorful version of the real-life saint, the way Odysseus is a literary representation of an actual voyager, or he may be more like Sinbad, a convenient character who could be used as the central figure in existing Irish sea sagas. These sagas are centuries old and concern, among other things, fairy lands and western voyages.

The historical Brendan, patron saint of Kerry, was born about 484 near Tralee. He was well educated, even for a priest, having studied mathematics, astronomy, Latin, and Hebrew. We know that he founded monasteries in western Ireland. We also know that he sailed to Wales, to the Hebrides off northern Scotland, and to Brittany, the part of France that juts out into the Atlantic. He revisited the Hebrides at the age of eighty, and died in 577, past the age of ninety.

The legendary Brendan, who sailed across the Atlantic Ocean to America, earning the name Brendan the Navigator, was probably created by Irish monks. He bears a strong relationship to heroes of early Celtic literature. In fact, we can better understand this Brendan if we look first at some early Celtic stories about fabulous voyages. The Celts were an ancient people of western Europe, particularly what are now France and the British Isles. They inhabited islands, peninsulas, and stormy coasts, and their bards were famous for colorful sea adventures.

One of the best of their tales, *The Voyage of Bran*, which dates from before 700, was composed at an Irish monastery. Bran is told of a strange land across the sea where there is no death or decay, just perpetual joy. He and a band of followers sail west to this Isle of Joy, experiencing a number of adventures on their way. When they return, they find they have been forgotten and are warned not to land. One sailor steps ashore and crumbles to dust. It seems that centuries have passed since they departed. Bran and his men sail off again and vanish.

Other poems, legends, and folk tales tell of the discovery and exploration of fancied wonderlands to the west. In many of them we can find things that relate to the legendary Brendan's voyages. The Welsh as well as the Irish told such travel stories. One Welsh legend tells how in 1170, King Madoc of North Wales launched an expedition to a vast land across the western sea. He left a hundred and twenty settlers behind in this land and returned to Wales for more. This time Madoc departed with ten ships and hundreds of colonists, but they were never heard from or seen again. There was a popular theory many years ago that the blue-eyed Mandan Indians of the Dakota region were descended from Madoc and his settlers.

The legendary St. Brendan probably owes more to this Celtic folk literature than to the exploits of the real Brendan, and more than likely he has had attached to him incidents from other people's travels. He has also become associated with obviously fictitious episodes; for example, the episode in which Brendan and his monks cook a meal on the back of a whale, which they have mistaken for an island, is straight out of the reservoir of seafarers' tales that supplied material for the Sinbad story.

The Irish monks who created the legendary Brendan were fond of adventure stories about quests in outer regions and fairy lands. The wove pagan folk material into their chronicles and held onto the classical belief that the earth is round. What is more, these unorthodox monks them-

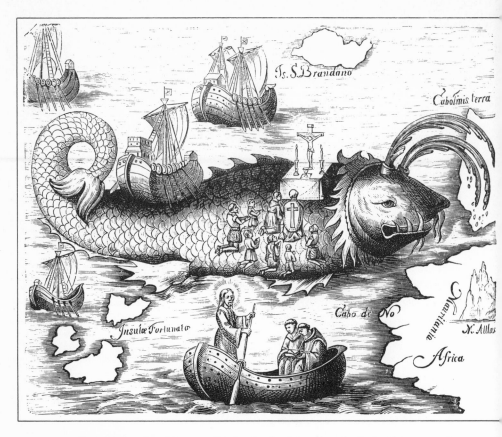

Brendan saying Mass on the back of a friendly whale. In this engraving made from an old miniature, Brendan's Isle can be seen at the top of the picture.

selves went sailing in the waters off northwestern Europe. Some of them sailed to the Orkneys, off the northern tip of Scotland. By the year 900, after the Norse invasions of Ireland, they had participated in voyages to Iceland. A monk named Cormac was supposedly blown off course northward for fourteen days. Clues in the story of this voyage suggest that he was actually blown to Greenland.

These men wrote about Brendan the Navigator long after the real saint's own lifetime. Brendan first appears as a mighty voyager in Adamnan's *Life of St. Columba,* (c.680) which also contains the story of Cormac's northern voyage. The abbot Adamnan, another scholar and traveler, was born about fifty years after Brendan's death. However, some of his stories had been told and sung over and over long before he wrote them down. So the legendary Brendan may have been taking shape during the real saint's lifetime.

Adamnan wrote about Brendan late in the seventh century. In the literature of the next century we find references to Brendan "sailing the sea" and "seeking the Land of Promise." The whale episode was added to the legend in that century and more details accumulated in the ninth. It was not until the tenth century that a biography of St. Brendan finally appeared. It was followed shortly after by a separate work, *Navigatio Sancti Brendani,* an account of his great voyage. The *Navigatio,* which is a travel story with Brendan as the central figure, probably dates from between 900 and 920. It is a narrative filled with marvelous details, magical episodes, repetition, and mystic numerology, and is considered an Irish *Odyssey.*

The *Navigatio* tells how Brendan goes to sea after hearing about the Land of Promise. He and a group of monks build a "curragh" or coracle, a small, slightly rounded craft with ribs covered by greased hides. After sailing in it for forty days they manage to land on a steep, rocky island. At first they find only an abandoned house, but finally meet one local inhabitant. Next they sail to the Isle of Giant Sheep, and winter there. It is on Easter Sunday that they cook breakfast on the small island that turns out to be a whale. After this they return to the Isle of Giant Sheep, then proceed to a nearby island called the Paradise of Birds. A talking bird tells Brendan that the birds on the island are

Four early woodcuts depicting scenes from Brendan's voyage.

all lost souls. He also says that Brendan and his companions, who have been away from home for a year, will continue their travels for six more years.

After leaving the Paradise of Birds they are tossed on the sea for three months. At last they come to the Island of St. Ailbe, which is inhabited by Irish monks. Other adventures follow and lead them to a "thick" sea, where they drift until a wind blows them back to the Isle of Giant Sheep. They voyage among islands now familiar to them and finally sail west for forty days. Brendan and his monks witness a battle between a whale and a large sea monster. They are trapped on an island by storms and after three months finally sail north. The travelers come to a large, flat island on which grow big purple fruits, each yielding a pound of juice. Then, after many days, sometimes fasting and sometimes being fed by a beautifully plumed bird who drops grapes to them as big and red as apples, they come to an island covered with grapes. Brendan and his monks stay on the island for forty days. In departing they manage to escape from a gryphon, the fabulous beast with the head and wings of an eagle and the body of a lion.

Their adventures are not over. They sail into a clear sea where they can see the fish below the surface of the water. The fish come up and circle the boat when Brendan says Mass. Next the wanderers come to an enormous floating column of crystal and an island of giant smiths who throw burning slag at them. Another island they pass contains a smoking mountain. They come to a rocky islet inhabited by a hermit named Paul, who says he is the man who buried St. Patrick. During Lent of the final year of their voyage they sail south. They celebrate Easter on the back of the friendly whale on whose back they had cooked that first Easter at sea. He carries them back to the Paradise of Birds. Finally, they sail for another forty days and reach the Land of Promise that first lured Brendan into making the voyage.

In the Land of Promise they explore the country for forty days without seeing its far side, which suggests that it was really a continent. The travelers come upon a great river, and then a young man appears who tells them to turn back. The young man explains that Christ made Brendan wander for seven years so that he could see the mysteries of the ocean; but now his voyage is over. Brendan's successors, says the young man, will rediscover the Land of Promise many years later in a time of trouble. And so, with some stops on the way, Brendan and his monks return home.

Did the Irish Discover America?

The story related in the *Navigatio* is essentially the same as that in the popular oral legend. There are two voyages according to the legend, but a curious break in the *Navigatio* indicates that it is really two continuous narratives with a connecting midsection. The recurring use of the number forty in the *Navigatio* is meant to be symbolic, rather than an accurate measure of time. Forty days was a time span with strong religious meaning for early Christians. The forty days of Lent reminds us that this early heritage is still with us. In the same way, seven was a mystic number and remains a "lucky" number to this day. The repetition of various incidents and places, however, is not mystical or religious. Repetition is a storytelling device we often find in stories that were spoken or sung. Repeated features tend to stick in the memories of listeners.

Some modern scholars believe that Brendan's voyage can be explained in terms of the geography of the Atlantic Ocean. In the early 1960's Geoffrey Ashe, an author who later studied the sites associated with King Arthur, sailed over what he believes to be Brendan's route. In his book

Land to the West, Ashe charts a truly fascinating journey. Some of his interpretations of the material in the *Navigatio* are shared by other experts.

The Isle of Giant Sheep and the Paradise of Birds have been associated with the Faeroes, Danish islands halfway between Britain and Iceland. Their name is derived from the Danish word for sheep. One of the islands, Vagar, is filled with migratory birds from spring through summer. In addition, the waters around the Faeroes are filled with whales.

The island of giant smiths suggests a volcanic eruption. The episode reminds us of the one in which Polyphemus hurls a boulder at Odysseus; this is also taken to be a description of a volcano erupting. In the legend of St. Brendan it is followed by an even clearer description of another volcano—the smoking mountain. These scenes bring to mind the coast of Iceland, and the recent emergence of the volcanic island of Surtsey out of the sea off Iceland serves to strengthen, if not confirm, this belief. The column of crystal, which takes Brendan four days to sail around, must be an iceberg. On the other hand, the clear sea with visible fish suggests to Ashe the waters of the Bahamas, three thousand miles to the southwest. If this seems strange, though the description fits, Ashe believes that Brendan's voyage did indeed cover thousands of miles.

Let us briefly join Ashe as he follows the sailing saint. He says that Brendan's boat was built at Brandon Creek in the Dingle Peninsula of western Ireland. From there Brendan and the monks sailed to St. Kilda in the Outer Hebrides and then to the Faeroes. But then Ashe moves them far to the southwest, to Madeira or the Canary Islands or the Cape Verde Islands. Medieval maps showing "Brendan's (or Brandan's) Isle" usually place it in that general area. He believes St. Ailbe is Madeira, four hundred miles west of

Africa, and that Brendan went from there to the Azores, a thousand miles west of Portugal. The "thick" sea they reach after that is, he says, the Sargasso Sea. According to Ashe's interpretation, Brendan spends each Christmas in Madeira and each spring back in the Faeroes.

The next part of the voyage takes Brendan past Iceland and Greenland. The natives he meets, says Ashe, must be eskimos. In the life of Brendan there is an account of his northern voyage, and it includes the description of a sea cat. This, Ashe feels, is clearly a walrus. We are now in what, according to the biography and the popular legend, is Brendan's second voyage. Ashe places the saint in the Bahamas at this point, possibly at Grand Cayman or Jamaica. The surfacing fish, he says, may be the dolphins or sailfish of Bimini.

Back north we go. The fiery, hellish island of the giant smiths, is Iceland. Ashe sees a reference to the volcanic Mt. Hekla, and locates the second volcano farther north, on Jan Mayen, an island between Norway and Greenland, northeast of Iceland. Its principal feature is Beerenberg, a 7,000-foot volcanic mountain. Paul's retreat is Rockall, beyond the Hebrides but south of Iceland. Brendan's final journey, according to Ashe, leads from the Faeroes past Iceland and Greenland. It continues down to Newfoundland, past Nova Scotia, to the Atlantic coast of what is now the United States. Ashe thinks it could even have continued down to Chesapeake Bay and inland, over the Appalachians, to the Ohio River.

To support this startling interpretation, Ashe relies on the scholarship of various authorities, but even more on the material in the story. Just from reading the *Navigatio*, he says, we can reconstruct its author's probable geographical knowledge. The prevailing westerlies, the Gulf Stream, Icelandic volcanoes, icebergs, Madeira, the Bahamas, Jamaica, and the foggy Grand Banks of Newfoundland are all indicated by descriptions in the text.

How far do the scholarly authorities support him? They believe the Irish of the tenth century knew the Faeroes and Iceland, possibly even St. Kilda and the iceberg zone to the north. But the Bahamas and the coast of North America remain questionable. Samuel Eliot Morison, in discussing Brendan, notes that not one single early Irish artifact has been found in North America.

Ashe computes a day's sail at from thirty-five to fifty miles. Allowing for some symbolism in the repetition of "forty days' sail," much of his interpretation is convincing. Such an enormous voyage in a skin boat is most unlikely, as Ashe admits. But the life of Brendan says the second voyage was made in a wooden ship. Two voyages in two vessels may simply have been combined for literary purposes. The first voyage, in waters close to Ireland, may have been the historical Brendan's. In the greater voyage the saint serves to personify Irish geographical lore in the tenth century.

The Brendan of the legends and the *Navigatio* is called upon by a divine voice to leave all his possessions and preach the word of God in a great, unknown land across the sea. He obeys the divine command and, after a long and difficult journey, reaches a land far to the west. There delicious wild vines, weighed down with grapes, grow in abundance. He passes a land of fogs and shoals, with waters populated by walruses, seals, and many fish, and continues south to a land of hostile, dark-skinned savages.

Can there be any question what this suggests? The similarity to the Vineland of the Vikings is striking; the apparent description of the Grand Banks of Newfoundland is uncanny. Did St. Brendan, or some Irish monks, reach the New World more than seven centuries before Columbus,

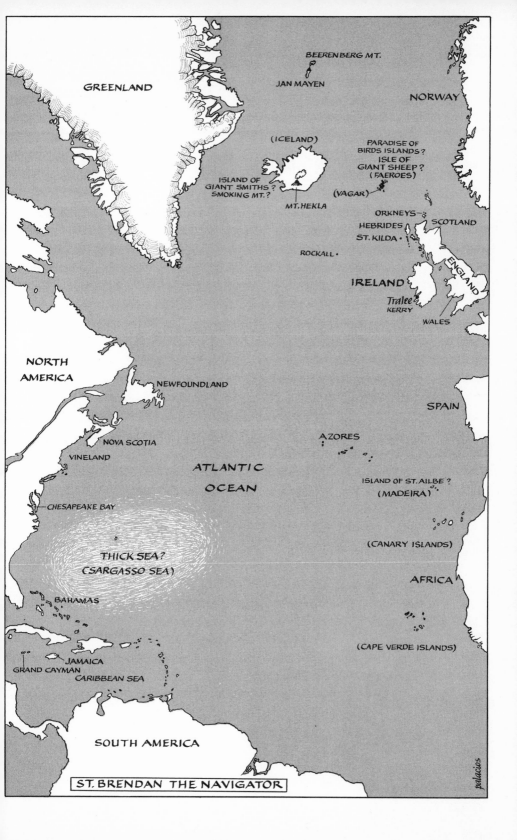

more than two hundred years before the Vikings? How else do we explain some of the details in the story? On the other hand, why have researchers found no early Irish relics in North America? The solid evidence St. Brendan left behind him exists in and around the British Isles. Beyond that we have only an island or islands bearing his name—a "flyaway" that never existed somewhere out in the Atlantic—a Neverland.

THREE

The Mysterious East

FROM the early Middle Ages right up to modern times, Europe has looked westward and eastward with what seem to be different eyes. The West has represented discovery, opportunity, and destiny. "Beyond the horizon," a phrase that implies no specific direction, somehow meant westward to Europeans. There was something optimistic and hopeful about the West. But Europeans felt differently about the East. From earliest times they have looked upon it as "the mysterious East."

Precisely the frame of mind that made the East "mysterious" also made it a Neverland; in fact, "the mysterious East" is the strangest Neverland we shall encounter. For one thing, there is no question that an East existed. But the East that lived in the minds of Europeans did *not* exist. It was filled with wonders and creatures of the imagination. Its geography was pure nonsense. At first, Europeans believed that Asia was smaller than Europe. When they reluctantly disabused themselves of this notion, they decided it was less populous, and they believed that India was attached to Africa. These and other absurdities made a real place into an imagined one—a Neverland. The closest modern parallel is the nineteenth-century immigrants' view of America, where the streets were said to be paved with gold.

More than anything else, the East was inaccessible—"attached" to Europe and inaccessible. We have only to consider Columbus, sailing across an ocean in an attempt to reach it, or Vasco da Gama, sailing all the way around Africa, to realize how inaccessible it was. But it was *there;* so it was as open to the imagination as it was closed to the traveler. Northward lay ice, southward lay deserts and jungles, and westward lay fog and ocean. But eastward lay land—a vast continent that grew with each infrequent, amazing report. In such a land who knew what wonders existed? It was fertile territory for a traveler willing to fill in his own details.

A distinction was usually made between the Near East, or Levant, and the Far East, or Orient. In travelers' terms the Levant meant the Holy Land and neighboring countries, as opposed to the more distant India and China. The Holy Land became a region of intense interest to a Christianized Europe, a goal of travelers even in an age when travel was exceedingly difficult.

Travelers to the Levant provided Europeans with most of their scanty knowledge of the outside world. In the fourth century a traveler named Silvia, probably St. Silvia of Aquitaine, recounted her journey to the Holy Land. Much later, a secondhand account of Bishop Arculf's tour of the Holy Land in 670 described many miraculous sites in and around Jerusalem. It also provided descriptions of Damascus, Alexandria, and Constantinople. There were, however, few such travelers. Much of the Levant was in the hands of Christian Europe's Islamic enemy, and the antagonism between the Greek and Roman churches separated eastern and western Europeans. Frankish settlements in Syria and Palestine, established as a result of the First Crusade, reopened contact between Europe and the Near East about 1100. For centuries this contact had been slight, troubled, and often interrupted. Nevertheless, it was more contact than Europe had with the Far East.

Some knowledge of India survived in the west after the era of Alexander the Great. When Alexander died in 323 B.C., his empire reached as far east as India. But the Roman Empire that followed was more European, and extended no closer to India than Mesopotamia. Nevertheless, the trade route across the Indian Ocean was open as late as the sixth century. It was then that Cosmas, known as "the Indian voyager," visited the Malabar coast. As for the rest of Asia, even though Chinese silk was sold in the Roman Empire, the areas north and east of India remained unknown. Knowledge of China was a virtual blank in Europe for most of the centuries before Marco Polo's visit.

In the seventh century, just before the rise of Islam cut off the land and sea routes to the East, Theophylactus Simocatta, a European, reported on what some envoys to Constantinople from a Turkish kingdom in central Asia had told him about China. Direct contact was nonexistent; the few Europeans who traded with the Far East did so through Arab middlemen. In the year 878 China closed its ports to all foreigners, though some Arabs continued to trade overland up to the country's borders. And in the twelfth century, Benjamin of Tudela, who traveled to Baghdad, Mosul and points up to the Chinese border, managed to pick up information about fellow Jews inside China.

In 1206 the Mongols united under Genghis Khan and began their conquest of the Eurasian continent. Soon all of this vast land area was under their domain except for India, Arabia, part of Indo-China, and western Europe. They controlled not only all of China, but countries as far west as Russia. The Europeans called them Tartars, mixing the name of one tribe, *Tatar*, with the classical name for hell, *Tartarus*. Within half a century they threatened to conquer the whole known world. In 1260 Pope Alexander IV called upon Christendom to unite to face the common enemy. But the Mongol threat lessened and Europe remained divided.

Meanwhile, there were contacts of a semidiplomatic nature by two Franciscan friars who made separate journeys to Karakorum. Giovanni de Piano Carpini was sent there in 1245 by Pope Innocent IV. Guillaume de Roubrouck (William of Rubrouck) was sent in 1253 by Louis IX of France. They returned with interesting accounts of their trips, but without any signs that Eastern rulers were willing to establish contacts. It was time for the merchants of Venice to move in and try.

Marco Polo

About the year 1260 two Venetian merchants, Niccolò and Maffeo Polo, sailed from Constantinople to Sudak in the Crimea. From there they traveled with a native caravan to the capital city of the Western Tartars, on the Volga River. In 1262 the local ruler, Barka Khan, went to war with the khan of the Levant. The warfare forced the Polos to move to another Tartar territory. They settled in Bukhara and stayed long enough to learn the language. Then the local khan sent them on a diplomatic mission to his overlord, Kublai Khan, in far off Cathay (China).

Kublai Khan administered a vast empire from his court at Khan-balik, modern Peking. More civilized than his

Marco Polo in an 1872 engraving, looking more like a nineteenth-century banker than a thirteenth-century merchant.

predecessors, he also differed from them in that he greeted the Westerners warmly. He even asked them to have their Pope send a special mission to teach Christianity to the Chinese. But the Polos, when they headed home in 1269, arrived in Acre to the news that there was no Pope. Clement IV had died the year before, and disputed elections would leave the church without a leader for three years. The Polos stayed in Italy until 1271, waiting for a new Pope to be elected so they could comply with Kublai Khan's request. Finally they left for Acre, where they picked up two friars, instead of the hundred Kublai had asked for. With these two churchmen and last-minute blessings and credentials from a newly elected Pope, they began their second journey to the Far East. Also accompanying them was Niccolò's seventeen-year-old son, Marco.

The Polos left Acre late in 1271 and remained out of contact with the West for more than twenty years. It was not until 1292 that they traveled homeward, accompanying an imperial party escorting a bride for the khan of the Levant. They were not back in Venice until 1295. But their return, and the subsequent publication of Marco's travel memoirs, marked a turning point in East-West relations. In the fourteenth century the church established missions in eastern China, and overland trade routes from Italy to China were firmly fixed.

Our interest in the Polos begins with their return home, when they added a major chapter to the story of the mysterious East. The account of their return home is a good one; however, it was added to the Marco Polo story more than two and a half centuries *after* the fact. By that time "Marco Million" had become almost as much a legend as a fact. The homecoming story was first told by the geographer Giambattista Ramusio, in the Preface to his 1553 printed edition of Marco's book. It has all the trappings of a fairy tale ending. The Polos, on their return, are not recognized by their family or friends. In fact, they are believed to be long dead. Moreover, these strangers are dressed in rags and hardly look like anyone's friends or relatives. But the travelers open up the Polo house and set up an enormous banquet, to which they invite all the Polo family members, friends, and neighbors. Then, at the height of the banquet, they rip open their shabby clothes and shower the table with emeralds, rubies, and diamonds. Naturally, after that, everyone recognizes them.

There is another Marco Polo story, equally entertaining, that is probably equally unreliable. On his deathbed, in 1324, when he is about seventy, Marco is asked if he wants to take back all those unbelievable things he told of in his travel book. His reply, according to the story, is that he hadn't even told all the wonders he had seen. If Marco didn't tell all in his book, however, it was not because he was holding anything back. Any omissions stem from the circumstances surrounding the writing and publication of the book.

In 1298 Marco Polo was a prisoner of war in Genoa, probably remaining in prison until the middle of 1299. To pass the time, he told stories of his travels to another prisoner, Rustichello of Pisa, a popular writer of romances. Together they fashioned the book that came to be known as *The Travels of Marco Polo.* Though they also worked from Marco's notes after their release from prison, much of the book is pure Rustichello. Scholars have determined this by comparing passages in the book with his earlier writings. But two important points should be kept in mind. One is that the descriptions are Marco's, and he was an excellent observer. The other is that Rustichello made the book a best seller. Few travel books even today can claim equal popularity or influence.

Manuscript copies of the book exist in several languages, but none is complete. Reconstructions made from various manuscripts are not complete either. Ramusio said that the original had been written in Latin, but modern scholars are almost certain it was written in French. The best manuscript, an early fourteenth-century French one, is known to be abridged. The fuller version printed by Ramusio is thought to contain material of his own invention along with some authentic material from a lost manuscript. Certainly some parts of the book have been lost. This may explain why Marco does not mention either tea or printing, both of which we would expect to find in an account of China. But what Marco does mention, or did originally, was enough to astound fourteenth-century Europe. And the book remains fascinating even for modern readers.

In the Prologue to his *Travels,* Marco Polo notes that people like to know about various races and the peculiarities of various regions of the world. They will find such things, he says, here in his book, told by someone who has seen them himself or heard of them from reliable sources. The book is accurate and free of fabrication; it contains nothing but the truth. Since Adam, he explains, there has been no man of any race or religion "who has known or explored so many of the various parts of the world and of its great wonders as this same Messer Marco Polo." For this reason it would be a great pity not to have a written record of all the things he saw or heard by true report, "so that others who have not seen and do not know them may learn them from this book." Even with this Prologue, many readers, though they were enthralled, were not willing to believe the wonders that the travelers encountered.

When the Polos left Acre in 1271 they set out for Hormuz, on the Persian Gulf. Their plan was to reach China by sea. But they changed this plan and headed north through Persia. They traveled all the way to Pamir, in western China north of the Himalayas. This region, first mentioned in Marco's book, was rarely entered again by Europeans until the nineteenth century. From Pamir they traveled eastward until they reached Khotan, crossing still other regions hardly explored until the nineteenth century. The next leg of their journey took them across the Gobi Desert. Early in 1275 they were cordially received by Kublai Khan in his palace at Shangtu. The name "Shangtu" is more familiar to us in the exotic variation used by the poet Samuel Taylor Coleridge:

In Xanadu did Kubla Khan
A stately pleasure dome decree. . . .

Settled in Cathay, Marco studied the language and soon entered public service. He was sent on official missions and traveled through various provinces of Kublai's domain, as far as Tibet and northern Burma. His detailed reports about the far reaches of the empire greatly interested Kublai Khan. Marco rose in the imperial service, and he and his family grew rich through the great Khan's favors. But they found no opportunity to leave China until 1286, and even then the trip was delayed for a few years. They finally sailed from Amoy, headed for Persia; but, because they were forcibly detained in Sumatra and India, the journey took them two years.

Both the popularity of Marco's book and the disbelief with which some people greeted it are understandable. The Polos were the first Europeans to travel across all of Asia and observe its people and places. Marco was the first traveler to describe the vastness of China and its riches, which seemed fantastic to fourteenth-century Europeans. He and his family were the first westerners to visit the emperor's court at Peking. The strange countries he described were part of an unbelievably far-reaching empire. It included not just what is now China, but also Tibet, Burma, and Thailand, as well as Sumatra and Japan.

The Travels of Marco Polo is divided between an account of the journey to Cathay and a description of Kublai's empire. Modern scholars agree that Marco was a good reporter. Perhaps for this very reason, his book could not remove the air of mystery surrounding the East. Even those who believed his story could not help being overawed by such a region. More than that, his audience, whether or not it believed Marco, was willing to believe a great deal about the Orient. It liked the idea of a mysterious East.

The popularity of the mysterious East was firmly established late in the fourteenth century by a traveler who may never have seen any of its marvels. The traveler wrote an enormously popular book that did much to strengthen Europe's belief in the fabulous wonders of the Orient. We know that Marco Polo's book was popular because more than eighty manuscript copies of it have survived. This other traveler's book survives in more than two hundred manuscript copies. And, like *The Travels of Marco Polo*, it is still in print in English and many other languages. The book might rival Marco's in reputation except for one thing—we know now that it is largely invention. In fact, even the name of the author, Sir John Mandeville, is an invention.

This interesting travel book was written in French and appeared sometime between 1357 and 1371. The first date marks the end of the travels described in the book; the second is that of the oldest known manuscript copy. The first English translation appeared early in the fifteenth century. In fact, the book was quickly translated into various languages and was extremely popular throughout all of Europe. It remains a fascinating book to read, being filled with many colorful details. But, like the Sinbad story, it is something of a grab bag. Modern scholars have been able to point out the different sources from which its details are drawn. And it has long been thought that its real author, or more properly its compiler, was a physician from the Flemish city of Liège. This man, Jean de Bourgogne, also known as Jean à la Barbe, arrived in Liège about 1343 and died there on November 17, 1372. Very little is known about him except that he apparently did some traveling in the Near East.

Sir John Mandeville taking leave of Edward III. This picture dates from the early fifteenth century, when Mandeville and his travels were very much believed in.

In the book Sir John Mandeville says he is an English knight who left St. Albans in 1322 and traveled to Turkey, Armenia, Tartary, Persia, Syria, Arabia, Egypt, Libya, Ethiopia, Chaldea, Amazonia, India, and the surrounding countries. He describes such places as Constantinople, Jerusalem, Mt. Sinai, and a Well of Youth at Polombe, which we know is Quilon on the Malabar Coast in southwest India. He tells how he served the sultan of Egypt and the emperor of China; how he took astronomical observations on a trip to Sumatra; and how he traveled through a haunted valley in Armenia. He also says that he returned home in 1357, after thirty-five years of energetic traveling, because he was afflicted with gout.

One of the main sources of the Mandeville material is the narrative written in 1330 by Friar Odoric of Pordenone. Odoric was a Franciscan monk who went to China in 1318 and traveled in the East for several years. Most of Mande-

ville's travels beyond the Hold Land—from Hormuz to India; on to the Malay Archipelago; from there to China; and back through western Asia—are taken from Odoric. The Odoric-Mandeville similarities were recognized quite early, and Mandeville, perhaps as a cover-up, even suggests that he traveled with Odoric. This untrue and improper suggestion was actually incorporated into later editions of Odoric's narrative. It is a measure of Mandeville's popularity that early commentators began to say that Odoric's narrative had been drawn from Mandeville's.

This much must be admitted. Mandeville's story is far more colorful and interesting than Odoric's. Whenever he misinterprets something from Odoric he turns it into something more imaginative. There is, for example, a colorful episode in the Valley Perilous. It is clearly expanded from material in Odoric's narrative, and just as clearly is better as a story. This episode is probably the source of John Bunyan's Valley of the Shadow of Death in his 1678 classic, *The Pilgrim's Progress.* Mandeville may be a fraud, but his popularity and influence surpassed those of the real travelers on whom he was based.

Even the parts of the Mandeville book on Egypt and the Holy Land, which might have been based on firsthand observations, have been questioned. It is thought that these parts derive from Wilhelm von Boldensele, a German knight who wrote of his travels in 1336. Much of the Asian history and geography is from Hetoum's *Historiae Orientis.* Hetoum was an Armenian monk who dictated the material in French, while he was at Poitiers in 1307. Most of the information on the Tartars comes from Carpini, the Pope's ambassador to Karakorum in 1245. Further information comes from the *Speculum historiale* of Vincent de Beauvais, another early traveler.

Oddly enough, there seems to be no borrowing from Marco Polo. One passage that could have been taken from

Marco's book could just as well have been taken from Odoric's narrative. Mandeville includes an account of Prester John and his fabulous realm, a Neverland we will look at in detail later. But Mandeville's account is similar to Marco's, Odoric's, and others of the time. In addition, the monsters and other wonders in Mandeville can be traced to Pliny and Solinus, classical Roman writers, or else to various medieval bestiaries and similar books.

The Mandeville book may neither be entirely borrowed nor fictitious. Some passages cannot be traced to any other source; the use of many unexplained Arabic words may stem from the author's own knowledge. On the other hand, these words may just represent mistakes in copying the manuscript. The author seems to have been more than just a storyteller, however. He believes in a spherical earth and says that ships may yet sail around the world. And he tells of a story heard in his youth of the man who traveled continually east and came to his own country again. He knows how to figure latitude by observing the pole star, and writes about the antipodes, inhabitants of a hemisphere opposite to his own. But in general, the Mandeville geography is very much in keeping with the times. The author believes, for example, that Jerusalem is situated at the center of the world. This is proved, he says, by the fact that a spear planted erect in Jerusalem on the day of the equinox casts no shadow at noon. Such an occurrence would be true, we should note, only if Jerusalem were situated on the equator.

Does it matter that Mandeville did not exist, or that his book is not original, just a collection of rewritten tales, a grab bag lifted from various medieval travelers? No, because through Mandeville the tales have grown richer. The author may or may not have been a traveler, but he was an excellent and imaginative writer. After six hundred years his book is still worth reading, and the search for fabled wonders in a fanciful Orient that continued into the eighteenth century is certainly a tribute to the success of Sir John Mandeville.

Wonders and Creatures of the East

There is no simple answer to why and how the East became mysterious. After all, Asia was more accessible to the early Mediterranean civilizations than most of Africa or even northern Europe. And westward lay an enormous fog-shrouded ocean. We cannot even say when it became mysterious. For convenience we can mention 327 B.C., the year Alexander the Great set out for India. But the land where the sun rose was considered special long before Alexander's time. For some ancient peoples the East was where Paradise was located. The mysterious East is an element in the Jason story. And Herodotus certainly contributed to the picture of an East that was filled with wonders.

When the Roman empire was at the height of its grandeur the world east of the empire had already taken on its mysterious air. Much of this was due to a writer named Arrian (c.95–175 A.D.). Arrian was a Greek who became an officer in the Roman army and later a consul in Cappadocia. He wrote seven volumes about Alexander and his campaign in India. A companion eighth volume concerned India itself and the voyage in Indian waters of Nearchus, one of Alexander's admirals. In addition, he wrote a book called *Periplus*, a geographical description of the Euxine (Black) Sea.

From Arrian we get some idea of how facts about the East grew into legends. His account of Nearchus' meeting with whales is clearly the basis for many future tall tales. Arrian tells us that Alexander, finding crocodiles in the Indus River, thought he had discovered the source of the Nile, the only river he knew that contained crocodiles. Alexander realized his mistake, but Arrian's story became

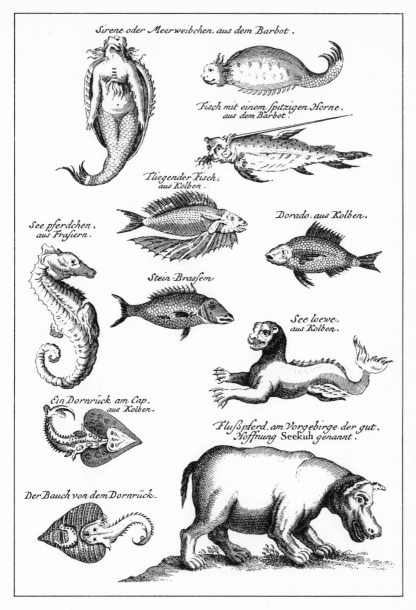

Fish and other wonders of the sea, including a Siren (upper left), as illustrated in a German book published as late as 1747.

the basis for one of the great misconceptions of medieval geography. For years it was thought that Africa and India were connected, and that the Erythraean Sea (Indian Ocean) was landlocked.

One of Arrian's principal sources of information about India was an earlier writer, Megasthenes. This Greek historian served as ambassador to an Indian king who ruled about 300 B.C. at his court on the Ganges River. Megasthenes' historical and geographical book on India is the principal early account we have of the country. It is also the source of one of the most intriguing, and most persistent, of all the fantasies associated with India—the story of giant gold-digging ants.

These ants, according to Megasthenes, were as big as foxes and had skins like panthers'. They lived in holes in the ground, piling up dirt around their entrances. The natives of the region sifted through the dirt and removed from it particles of gold, but they did so very secretly, because, according to Megasthenes, "if the animals notice it they pursue the fugitives and kill them and their draught animals." These ferocious ants probably grew out of exaggerated accounts of the marmot, a rodent that resembles the ground hog, woodchuck, or prairie dog. The marmot is quite harmless, so how can he have become such a dread killer? The explanation is simple enough: Anybody could steal the gold safely if it were dug up by harmless creatures, so the marmots became mankillers; but why they became ants is not certain.

Another popular but mythical feature of the Orient was the Mountain of Lodestone. It first appears in Ptolemy's *Geography*, in the second century A.D. In the Far East, near an island of Satyrs, says Ptolemy, is another island, a mountain of lodestone, which destroys ships by pulling out the nails that hold them together. A similar story appears in an eleventh-century Chinese book, where it is said to have been quoted "from an older book." The Mountain of Lodestone is obviously an enormous magnet. There is no evidence that sailors of the classical world knew about the magnetic compass. That marvelous invention came to the West much later; and it came from China, where the compass needle was magnetized by rubbing it with lodestone.

The magnetic mountain was a persistent myth, and it showed up as part of the medieval legends about Virgil. The Roman poet, who appears as a great magician in numerous medieval tales, supposedly gained his magic powers by sailing to a certain Magnetic Mountain. The Mountain of Lodestone is also mentioned by Idrisi. Its location is not clear, but it is presumably on the east coast of Africa. Later Arab geographers mentioned a mountain in eastern Africa rich in iron and lodestone, apparently magnetite. The mountain must have been the same one mentioned by Idrisi.

This marvelous feature of the eastern world "moved," as we have seen, from the Far East to Africa. Finally it moved out of the East altogether. In 1508 the cartographer Johannes Ruysch published a map showing an island with a Mountain of Lodestone in the Arctic Ocean, near the North Pole. Presumably Ruysch was offering an explanation of why compasses point north. But, as is so typical of Neverlands, we notice that facts don't necessarily replace fancies. The fabulous mountain moves as the eastern areas open up; it even takes on a logical reason for existing; but it doesn't disappear.

The Mountain of Lodestone also shows up in a medieval German romance called *Herzog Ernst von Schwaben* (Duke Ernest of Swabia). This story, probably written about 1160 by someone known as Heinrich von Veldeke, was loosely based on the career of an actual person. But the hero seems to have been combined with other historical figures, and the incidents of the story can be traced to various sources. One of the incidents appears in the Sinbad story, as we have mentioned. But we should add that the Duke Ernest story, like that of Sinbad, is something of a grab bag.

In the story, which is told in verse, Duke Ernest and his friend Wetzel journey to the Holy Land. After a storm at sea they land in "Grippia." There they fight the Agrippians, people with the heads and necks of birds. The men have the heads and necks of cranes, and the women those of swans. The Duke and Wetzel attempt to rescue a woman who says she is the "Princess of India." Because Grippia is supposed to be three days' sail from Syria, it has been suggested that its inhabitants are based upon pictures of the ibis-headed Egyptian god Thoth.

After this episode Duke Ernest's ship is attracted by the Mountain of Lodestone and wrecked. The Duke and Wetzel and two servants survive with the aid of gryphons, which reminds us of one of St. Brendan's adventures. Next they sail (like Sinbad) on a raft down a river that runs through a mountain and into a country filled with strange people. These people are quite remarkable, but they all come straight out of the more fanciful pages of Pliny's *Natural History*. Another episode, in which Pygmies battle cranes, can be traced to Homer. Pliny also mentions Pygmies, putting their height at twenty-seven inches. But Marco Polo later explained that these so-called Pygmies were monkeys, not men.

The author of the Duke Ernest romance presented the story as factual. We recognize it now as fancy; but its significance is that it is twelfth-century Europe's picture of the mysterious East. As such it makes clear that the East was a true Neverland. For at least two centuries more, despite Marco Polo, it remained so. Indeed, Marco Polo's descriptions served only to prove it was a fabulous region. Fact and fancy were separated by the thinnest of lines—a situation that can easily give rise to a Neverland.

Pliny's descriptions of monstrous people in faraway lands were still believed when this picture was printed in a German book in 1478.

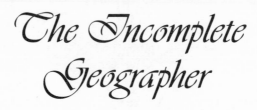

FOUR

The Incomplete Geographer

PRIMITIVE people usually picture the world as a flat disc under a hemispheric sky. Many ancient cultures adopted this world picture. The Egyptians, probably influenced by the long Nile valley, envisaged a rectangular earth and sky, something like a shoe box in shape. People usually picture themselves at the center of their world: We are most familiar with world maps that center on the United States; French schoolchildren study maps of the world that have Paris at the center; and we have already noted that medieval maps placed Jerusalem at the center of the world. Often in ancient times some major geographical feature was considered the world's center. For the Greeks it was sometimes Mt. Olympus, but more often it was a sacred rock at Delphi known as the "navel stone" of the world.

The Greeks took their geographical and astronomical concepts, including the heavenly constellations, from the Babylonians. The Greek world picture was developed between 600 B.C. and 550 B.C. by Thales of Miletus, who is also credited with being the first man to predict eclipses. A world picture is not necessarily a map; it is a concept. The early Greeks took up the Babylonian concept of the earth as a flat disc surrounded by an ocean. Anaximander of Miletus (611–547 B.C.), a contemporary of Thales, changed the disc to a drum. Other theorists proposed a flat, a saucer-shaped, or a cylinder-shaped earth. By the late fifth century B.C. most Greeks believed in a spherical earth. The man credited with introducing this concept—the earth as a globe— is the famous mathematician Pythagoras of Samos.

The great Greek philosophers Plato and Aristotle believed the earth was a globe; in fact, despite popular stories to the contrary, the idea persisted through all the centuries up to Columbus. The size of the globe, however, was a questionable item. It was measured with astonishing accuracy in the third century B.C. by Eratosthenes. His figure was expanded, then reduced and finally reduced further by the geographer Strabo. Ptolemy picked up Strabo's figure, and in time Columbus would make use of this incorrect measurement.

Maps had their place in the ancient world. The geometric measurement of land surfaces was important in Egypt to reestablish boundaries after the annual Nile floods. The Egyptians apparently also used maps as guides. Maps of the nether regions, drawn to aid the dead on their journey, have been found in Egyptian tombs. The Mesopotamians also had maps. An Assyrian clay tablet dating from about 500 B.C. contains a map of part of northern Mesopotamia, and later a Babylonian map of the world represents the earth as a circle surrounded by a sea and heavenly bodies.

Anaximander, according to tradition, devised the first Greek map in the sixth century B.C. He is also supposed to have created the first sundial and the celestial globe. The earliest Greek reference to a map appears in Herodotus, who tells how the Spartans are shown a bronze tablet inscribed with a picture of the whole earth, the sea, and all the rivers, but are not impressed by it. But their reaction was not typical, because we know that the early Greeks used maps.

What they used were maps of a special kind that would appear again in the Middle Ages. They relied mainly on

A twelfth-century map of the world showing three continents—Europe, Asia, and Africa. A note on the land to the right says: "There is a fourth quarter of the World, called the Antipodes, unknown to us because of the heat of the Sun."

written itineraries, but also had rough itinerary maps of their trade routes in the eastern Mediterranean. An itinerary is similar to the instructions we give to visiting friends or relatives—"turn right at the traffic light, go past the school on your right, after two more blocks you come to a gas station," and so on. The Trade routes followed coastlines, so itineraries took the place of marine charts. For early travelers they were probably more useful. In any case, there were no instruments for making the accurate measurements marine charts require.

Itinerary maps were also drawn for the principal inland trade routes. They often were drawn as straight lines, which eventually became what we now know as parallels and meridians. There was a north-south line corresponding to the Nile, and an east-west one for the trade route to Susa. The Mediterranean became fixed as an east-west body of water. But, just as trade routes became straight lines, coastlines tended to be flattened out. The Mediterranean Sea was pictured wider (east-west) and narrower (north-south) than it actually was. This distortion, which pushed Asia far to the east, also figured in Columbus' calculations.

The Greeks introduced one of their favorite ideas, symmetry, into their world picture. Geographical features of the North were balanced by those of the South, and likewise for the East and West. The shape of their world map was perfectly circular, with the center at Delphi. This, of course, was only a way of representing the earth's true shape, that of a globe. The next step was to divide the globe into meaningful units, and they arrived at 360 degrees. Each degree was equal to the circumference of the earth divided by 360. But how big was the circumference of the earth? Or, to put it another way, how many miles were in 1 degree? That was the problem solved by Eratosthenes.

The Greek scholar Eratosthenes (275–195 B.C.) was a

master of history, geography, astronomy, geometry, philosophy, grammar, and poetry. He was the author of books on many subjects, and is considered the founder of scientific geography. To calculate the circumference of the earth, Eratosthenes used a stick and an item of information. The information was that the sun shone down to the very bottom of a deep well in Syene at noon on midsummer day. In other words, the sun was vertical at Syene (modern Aswan) at that time; thus, an upright stick placed in the ground would cast no shadow. At precisely noon on midsummer day Eratosthenes conducted an experiment in Alexandria. He placed a stick upright in the ground and measured the angular distance of the sun; that is, he measured the degree of shadow, what portion of a full circle, his stick cast in Alexandria.

With this figure he could proceed with his calculations. He already knew the distance from Syene to Alexandria. Dividing the distance, which the Greeks measured in stadia, by the number of degrees of shadow, he calculated the number of stadia in 1 degree. Then, multiplying by 360, he arrived at a figure of two hundred and fifty-two thousand stadia for the circumference of the globe, which comes out to be a little under twenty-five thousand miles. Eratosthenes' figure is about fifty miles off the modern calculation. He said that 1 degree equals 68.5 miles, a remarkably accurate figure. Unfortunately, this figure was either not accepted or was quickly forgotten. At any rate, later geographers seem to have ignored it.

Eratosthenes was the first geographer to rough out latitude and longitude on a map. One axis of his map ran through the Mediterranean, from Gibraltar to Messina to Rhodes, and on eastward. The other ran from the mouth of the Don River, through Rhodes, to Alexandria, Aswan and points south. The successors to Eratosthenes criticized his maps. His chief critic was Hipparchus, a Greek astronomer and mathematician born about 190 B.C. Hipparchus, who also invented trigonometry and catalogued some eight hundred fixed stars, corrected Eratosthenes' map and compiled his own table of latitudes.

By the end of the second century A.D. the scientific geography of Eratosthenes was being abandoned. This was the time when Arrian's books were shaping the picture of the East. Some of Arrian—what he took from Megasthenes—is pure fancy; but what he took from Nearchus is pure fact. Nearchus had commanded Alexander's fleet on its voyage from the Indus River to the mouth of the Euphrates in 326 B.C. The fleet traveled along the southern coasts of what are now Pakistan and Iran and up the Persian Gulf. It was a twelve-hundred-mile journey; and, at an average of thirty miles a day plus many stops, it took Nearchus five months. He kept a log of the entire voyage, and it is this log that Arrian, in the second century A.D., added to his account of Alexander's career.

Some of the details from Nearchus' log have been confirmed by modern voyagers. Is Nearchus less reliable because incidents from his log reappear in the story of Sinbad? Nearchus' voyage is a fact; Arrian published his log as authentic. Nevertheless, it is also a fact that his description of the Europeans' first encounter with whales is the source of many fanciful tales.

The Remarkable Phoenician Voyagers

Much more than Eratosthenes' calculations was forgotten by the later classical world. By the time Prince Henry sent his Portuguese sailors around Africa, it had been forgotten that the Phoenicians, the greatest sailors before Columbus, had traveled the same waters long before. For example, the

long-standing belief that the Indian Ocean was landlocked
is a denial of one of the exploits of the Phoenicians.

About two centuries before Nearchus, early in the fifth
century B.C., one of the most remarkable Phoenician voyages took place. It was a voyage that, nearly two thousand
years later, fearful Portuguese sailors would repeat—a short
step at a time. The voyage was led by Hanno the Cartha-
ginian, and Carthage was a Phoenician settlement. It is recorded in a narrative known as the *Periplus*, which means
"circumnavigation." (The title is misleading because the
narrative describes coasting along the northern and western
shores of Africa, and Hanno probably did not circum-
navigate the continent.) The narrative, supposedly written
by Hanno himself and recorded in bronze in a temple at

Phoenician ships in an illustration taken from an Assyrian relief.
Though one has a mast, both are rowed by two banks of oars.

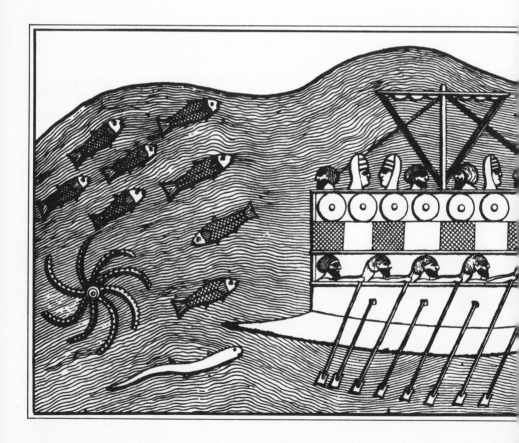

Carthage, is known to us in a Greek version that was circulated long after the voyage. But, like Nearchus' log, it is a travel report that modern research has confirmed.

The two most interesting features of the narrative are quite comprehensible to modern observers, however strange they must have seemed to the ancients. The first, a country full of fire, is described by Hanno this way: ". . . throughout each night we saw the land full of flames; in the midst of them was a very tall flame that towered above the other flames and seemed to reach up to the stars. By day we saw it was a very high mountain . . ." This awesome sight, clearly a volcano, Hanno named "the Chariot of the Gods."

After sailing past the burning land, Hanno says: ". . . we arrived at a bay called the Southern Horn, at the bottom of which lay an island full of savage people, the greater part of whom were women, whose bodies were hairy and whom

our interpreter called Gorillae. Though we pursued the men we could not seize any of them, but all fled from us, escaping over the precipices and defending themselves with stones. Three women were, however, taken, but they attacked their conductors with their teeth and hands, and could not be prevailed upon to accompany us. Having killed them, we flayed them and brought their skins to Carthage."

This remarkable account of meeting with gorillas, in which the apes are thought to be people, is not an isolated ancient fancy. We know that the Old Man of the Sea in the Sinbad story is thought to be an orangutan, and as late as the eighteenth century orangutans were still believed to be a species of man. The famous naturalist Linnaeus (1707–1778) called the orangutan a "wild man of the woods, that is, a second species of man, also called night man." But in 1847 something happened that indicated even more strongly that Hanno's narrative was not simply a sailor's yarn. That year the Gabon gorilla was discovered, an anthropoid ape corresponding exactly to Hanno's description, and found in the right place.

These and other passages in the text indicate that Hanno sailed along Africa's western shores. The Chariot of the Gods is most probably Mt. Cameroon, a 13,353-foot peak just in from the coast less than 5 degrees north of the equator. So Hanno may have reached the equator before meeting the gorillas and turning back. It was a remarkable voyage, and a stunning display of Phoenician seamanship.

An even more remarkable voyage took place earlier in the same century. The Egyptian Pharaoh, Necho II, who ruled from 609 B.C. to 594 B.C., ordered a circumnavigation of Africa. The voyage was undertaken by a Phoenician (or possibly an Egypto-Phoenician) crew. Herodotus provided an account of it about a hundred and fifty years afterward. He also noted that Africa, except for the part touching Asia at the Sinai Peninsula, "is surrounded on all sides by the sea." This fact, lost to later geographers, was demonstrated by Necho's sailors. Necho had just given up trying to build a canal from the Nile to the Red Sea when he equipped the expedition to sail around Africa. His instructions were that the expedition should return to Egypt through the Pillars of Hercules and across the Mediterranean Sea. The fact that Necho knew the expedition could return from the west suggests an even earlier circumnavigation.

The Phoenicians, Herodotus tells us, sailed into the Indian Ocean and then into the southern sea. In autumn they landed, tilled the fields, waited for the harvest, and then sailed on. In this way, he says, "after two years, they sailed through the Pillars of Hercules, and so returned to Egypt again in the third year." His concluding comment about the voyage is now seen as confirmation of its having taken place. "They related," says Herodotus, "which I cannot myself believe, though perhaps some other may, that as they rounded Libya [his name for Africa] they beheld the sun on their right hand." He did not believe such a peculiar fact; anybody living north of the equator probably wouldn't. However, if the Phoenicians sailed around Africa in a clockwise direction, when they were south of the equator and were facing west the sun *would* appear on their right, that is to the north. The part of the story Herodotus found unbelievable serves to convince us that the voyage actually took place. About six hundred years after Herodotus, his knowledge of the shape of Africa was not shared by geographers. The geographical data hard-won by the Phoenicians was lost until the Portuguese inched their way around Africa.

The Phoenicians were masters of the ancient seas, particularly those waters beyond the Pillars of Hercules. But just how far into the Atlantic did they sail? Did they, as some people insist, actually cross the ocean? Records indicate that they sailed the Atlantic near the coastlines of

Europe and Africa. They journeyed as far north as Britain and as far south as West Africa, but generally close to the land. We are quite certain they reached the Canary Islands and Madeira, and probably the Azores, though not on a regular basis. Medieval voyagers to the Canaries found the islands inhabited by cave dwellers known as Guanches. These people, living in a stone age culture, may have been the remnants of a Phoenician colony.

Phoenician ships were probably not capable of making a transatlantic voyage. Viking ships, which were similar, made the crossing, but by the much shorter northern route—their longest stretch of open water was between Greenland and Canada. Arguments for a Phoenician crossing of the Atlantic rest on somewhat shaky evidence, such as classical references to masses of seaweed outside the Pillars of Hercules. These references are taken to be descriptions of the Sargasso Sea. How could the classical world know about the Sargasso Sea unless someone had seen it? And who was more likely to reach it than a Phoenician sailor?

The argument is far from foolproof. What is meant by "outside" the Pillars of Hercules? The Sargasso Sea, between Bermuda and the West Indies, is closer to New York than to Gibraltar. This mass of floating seaweed, often pictured as an impenetrable graveyard of ships, is actually more terrible in fiction than in fact. The first real report we have of it comes from Columbus. It is not like the obstruction described in the classical accounts, and we cannot link it to the Phoenicians with any certainty.

The Curious World of Pliny and Ptolemy

Gaius Plinius Secundus, better known as Pliny the Elder, was a man of enormous energy and intellectual curiosity who constantly kept himself busy. Born about A.D. 23, he was trained in literature and the law. He also engaged in military and government service and was a friend of more than one Roman emperor. Most of his writings have been lost, but we know that he produced books on military science, grammar, oratory, biography, and over fifty volumes of history. His *Natural History*, in thirty-seven books, is his most famous work. It covers such topics as cosmology, geography, physiology, zoology, botany, medicine, metallurgy, and the history of art. By modern standards it is an unscientific and superficial work, filled with errors and often boring. But it remains our major source of information about Roman art, science, and technology—in short, Roman civilization.

Pliny died in the eruption of Vesuvius (A.D. 79), a scientific observer to the very last. While sailing nearby he saw the smoke from the volcano and went to investigate. He dictated his observations under a shower of stones and returned to the safety of his ship. The next day, despite earth tremors and an enveloping darkness, he covered his head and went ashore to investigate further. He was asphyxiated by sulfur fumes, a martyr to his boundless energy and curiosity.

It is from Pliny that medieval Europe derived much of its idea of the "mysterious" East. He compiled a great deal of information about the Orient, much of it from Greek sources he did not fully trust. Oddly enough, though he expressed his doubts, he apparently was unable to separate fact from fiction. He picked up information from Homer and Herodotus, some of it pure legend, and then added his own fancies to it. The story of the gold-digging ants is typical Pliny. Much of what he considered fact is pure fiction—savages whose feet are turned backwards, natives of the area around the Black Sea with double sets of eyes, or people who cannot sink in water.

The best explanation of Pliny's inaccuracies is that he was not critical enough in accepting his sources of information. He noted, for example, that India "abounds in wonders." But his information came from an ancient Persian book on India that was filled with fancies. Later Roman and medieval writers used Pliny as a major source of information, usually repeating his fancies while discarding his facts. An encyclopedia of natural history written a thousand years later by a monk named Thomas of Cantimpre contains a "Book of Monstrous People of the East." It is simply an elaborate retelling of Pliny's marvels. We can see Pliny's lasting influence in Schedel's *World Chronicle,* published in 1493. Many of its fantastic descriptions are right out of Pliny's *Natural History.*

In India, says Schedel, there are men with dogs' heads who talk by barking, eat birds, and wear animal skins. Others have only one eye in the middle of their foreheads, and eat only animals. In Libya, meaning Africa, people are born without heads, but have mouths and eyes. Others are of both sexes, their right sides being male and their left sides female. Somehow they are able to bear children. Near Paradise, on the Ganges River, are men who eat nothing.

A Sicilian Cyclops, Ethiopian troglodite, and Indian satyr (LEFT)*, and a hairy aborigine* (ABOVE)*; described by Pliny and still sought by New World explorers when this woodcut was printed in 1653.*

Their mouths are so small they can sip only liquids through straws. They live on the juice of apples and flowers, and bad smells practically kill them. Then too, there are people with flat faces, without noses. Many have no tongues, and others have such large underlips they can cover their whole faces with them.

In a land Schedel calls Sicilia people have such large ears they can cover their whole bodies with them. In Ethiopia many people walk bent over like cattle, and others live for four hundred years. Many have horns, long noses, and goat's feet. In the western part of Ethiopia there are people with a single large foot who are so swift they can run as fast as wild animals. Other inhabitants of this region have four eyes. In the land of Scythia people have human forms and horses' feet. And in a land called Eripia live beautiful people with the necks and bills of cranes. In India, says Schedel, quoting Alexander the Great, there are men with six hands.

The description concludes with a discussion of the antipodes and why people on the opposite side of the earth don't fall off. "It would be contrary to nature," says Schedel, "for them to fall off . . . the things of the earth cannot fall away from, but only towards, the earth to which they belong." This final note sounds reasonable after the marvels derived from Pliny. And yet we can see the actuality from which some of the marvels arose. The flat faces of some Africans, the enormous lips of the Ubangis, need no explanation. The Scythian centaurs are merely an exaggerated account of a people who constantly lived, ate, and even slept in the saddle. Alexander's six-handed Indians bring to mind representations of the Indian deity Siva. Pliny and his copiers for a thousand years were content to record wonders without really examining them.

Even more influential than Pliny, because he shaped

A nineteenth-century French artist's examples of various antipodes— people on opposite sides of the earth. Spain is opposite New Zealand, Japan is opposite Argentina, etc.

the picture of the whole universe, was the Greek astronomer Ptolemy. Claudius Ptolemaeus, to give him his Latin name, lived in Alexandria in the second century A.D. His description of how the sun, moon and planets all moved around a stationary earth first appeared in his *System of Mathematics*. This work summarizes all the astronomical knowledge of Ptolemy's day. More important, it survived the fall of Rome and was translated into Arabic, forming the basis of all astronomical theory until Copernicus.

Ptolemy was more than an astronomer. As a mathema-

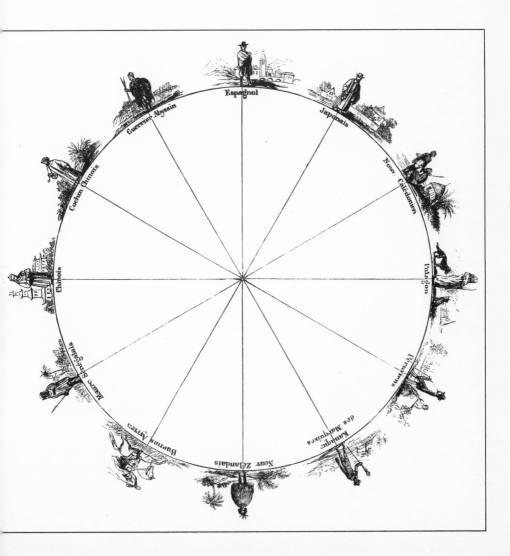

tician he developed, along with Hipparchus, the study of trigonometry. He wrote numerous scientific works, including a *Geography*. Even more than Eratosthenes and Hipparchus, it is Ptolemy who established the custom of fixing geographical positions by referring to their latitude and longitude. His *Geography* lists the positions of all the principal places in the known world. Ptolemy's surviving works include maps, which are either his own or very accurate copies of his originals. It is believed that most, if not all, were added to the books afterward. The oldest existing Ptolemaic manuscript dates from the twelfth century, a thousand years after his lifetime. But Ptolemy is credited with having produced a world map, drawn on a conic projection, twenty-six regional maps and sixty-seven maps of smaller areas. These last were drawn on a rectangular projection, which he approved of for smaller areas.

Though astronomy remained fixed for centuries by Ptolemy's ideas, his maps had no influence in Europe until the fifteenth century. His theories were spread through his *System of Mathematics*, which the Arabs called the *Amalgest*, the "Great Work." But it was only in the fifteenth century that the Europeans translated his books into Latin. Thus his influence as a geographer began just before the great age of discovery. As with his astronomy, it was not entirely a good influence. Ptolemy gave the length of 1 degree as 56.6 miles, rather than the more accurate 68.5 miles of Eratosthenes. Because he gave all his measurements in degrees, he overestimated the size of continents relative to the whole globe. In addition, his Mediterranean Sea extends 62 degrees of longitude, rather than the actual 42 degrees; he misrepresented the shape of the Indian subcontinent and overestimated the size of Ceylon; and worst of all, he had southern Africa extend eastward, locking in the Indian Ocean.

The Ptolemaic world system—spheres within spheres, all the way to the Primum Mobile, which the medieval world added as the "prime mover" of the other spheres.

Ptolemy's errors, and those of the Arabs, played a decisive role in Columbus' calculations. The Arabs kept classical Greek science alive, and spread it to Spain and southern Europe with the Moorish conquests. But they also conducted their own scientific experiments. When Harun al-Rashid's son became Caliph, nearly a thousand years after Ptolemy, he sent out surveyors to measure the earth. Using devices not available to Eratosthenes, they simultaneously shot the sun from two distant points. In essence they were really repeating his experiment. Unfortunately, they arrived at a figure of 76.4 miles per degree, slightly more than seven miles too great. The 76.4 figure was recorded by Alfraganus, an Arab scholar, and introduced into western Europe by Roger Bacon. Just to complicate matters, the Arab mile is more than one-and-a-third of our miles.

Columbus used the calculations of the Arabs, Ptolemy and others to plot his voyage to the Indies. But, to suit his purposes, he altered the various figures he used. For one thing, he substituted the short Roman mile for the Arab mile when using Arab figures. For another, he used the widest distances on the Ptolemaic maps, all inaccurately wide to begin with. In this way, he arrived at a distance of 14,700 miles from the west coast of Europe to the east coast of China. Then he took Ptolemy's inaccurate measure of the earth's circumference, which was 18,800 miles. Thus, the ocean between these two coasts came out to be about 4,000 miles wide. No wonder, on October 12, 1492, he believed he had crossed to the Indies.

FIVE

A Globe
with Corners

E VEN though we know the earth is round, we speak of the earth's "far corners," or of "the ends of the earth," a phrase equally inappropriate to a globe. We continue to use these phrases, knowing they are not accurate, because they are wonderfully expressive of great distance.

Our interest in ends and corners of the earth comes from our knowledge that these were among the fabulous places of the ancient, classical, and medieval worlds. They were largely unreachable, and being unreachable is one characteristic of Neverland. One aspect of geography before Columbus was its incompleteness; another was the vague awareness of lands beyond the known world. With so little of the world known, including some parts that had been forgotten, the belief in unknown distant lands was a powerful stimulus toward the creation of all sorts of Neverlands.

The classical world was closely bound to the Mediterranean Sea. The Roman Empire stretched nearly three thousand miles from west to east, from Spain to the borders of Armenia. But, with the exception of northern Gaul and

Britain, its frontiers were largely within three hundred miles of the Mediterranean. The earlier Greek world was equally bound to the Aegean Sea, a northern pocket of the Mediterranean, and to Asia Minor in the east. Alexander the Great extended his empire as far east as India, but that did not remain intact for long. We can get an idea of how limited the classical world was by noting that Malta, just south of Sicily, was often referred to as "the navel of the ocean."

Much of the Greek *Oikoumene*, or known world, was visited by Herodotus, the traveling Greek historian of the fifth century B.C. who described it in some detail. Though he was writing history, Herodotus put a lot of geography and anthropology into his book. He saw for himself a great many of the people, places, and things he told about. Born in Halicarnassus, in Asia Minor, Herodotus traveled in Europe, Asia, and Africa, visited Greece and its neighboring countries; toured Asia Minor, and eastward into Asia nearly as far as Susa; traveled through the islands of the eastern Mediterranean; explored Egypt as far up the Nile as Elephantine, an island at the first cataract, near modern Aswan; and reached the Caucasus Mountains and the mouth of the Danube River to the north.

Herodotus visited and described the magnificent city of Babylon and the pyramids of Egypt. His account of the "Tin Islands" is vivid enough to suggest that he journeyed past the Pillars of Hercules to Britain. His description of the trade route north from the Black Sea—from Pontus northeast to the Don and Volga rivers and along the Volga to Selonus at the junction of the Kama River—has been confirmed by modern scholars. The world described in the *Histories* of Herodotus, much of it at firsthand, spilled out beyond the *Oikoumene*. But it remained a factual world and did not include any fabulous "far corners."

Nevertheless, the Greeks, and the Romans after them, spoke of places beyond the known world. There were the Blessed Isles to the west, Ultima Thule to the north, and a great unknown southern continent. We have already seen that India, to the east, had passed out of the known world by Roman times, into a realm of fancy. The other extremities—the far western, northern and southern corners of the world—were fabulous places at the ends of the earth, but, because they were specific places, modern scholars have been able to identify or otherwise explain them with some certainty.

Ultima Thule

Let us begin with the most specific of the extremities. The northern terminus of the classical world was a place called Ultima Thule. In the first century A.D. Pliny wrote: "The outermost of all known lands is Thule." At the time of the summer solstice, "there are no nights there. In winter the day lasts only a short time, whereas the nights are very long." Two centuries later Solinus rewrote Pliny's *Natural History* and added some details to the picture of Thule. Both accounts, however, probably stem from the work of a much earlier Greek, Pytheas.

The Roman historian Tacitus (A.D. c.55–117), described northern Europe in his book *Germania*. In this work he refers to "another sea" to the north, presumably the Arctic Ocean. Again the source of this information may be Pytheas. Other references lead back to this Greek, the only known voyager to the north in ancient times who left a record of his travels. Pliny's account of amber in his *Natural History* repeats what Pytheas reported. He places the source of this mineral on an island called Abalus, which is almost certainly Heligoland, in the North Sea.

Who was Pytheas? His major work, *On the Ocean,* has been lost, but we know he was a geographer and a student of tides. Later writers quote his assertion: "the flood tide is caused by the waxing, the ebb tide by the waning moon." In 325 B.C. he left Massilia, modern Marseilles, to explore the Tin Islands (Britain) and the Gulf of Metuonis, the present Bay of Heligoland. These regions were important to the classical world as a source of tin, gold, and amber.

Pytheas journeyed overland to Corbilo, a port near modern St. Nazaire on the Bay of Biscay, a town that was gone by Caesar's time. From there he sailed to Albion (Britain), which he circumnavigated and may have explored by land. Most of the time he was very busy studying tides. He also journeyed to the Shetland Islands, north of Scotland, and sailed for six days across the North Sea to Thule. Just where that northern extremity was is not certain. Pytheas probably reached Norway, perhaps near the Trondheim Fjord, about 64 degrees north. Thule was supposed to be an island, but this does not rule out Norway. In Pytheas' time, and for centuries afterward, all of Scandinavia was believed to be an island.

So the northern extremity was an actual place, with a specific name. We may only be guessing that it was Trondheim, but it was *some place* that a traveler could visit and write about. This is an important distinction, because the western extremity also had a specific name. The difference, however, is that the western end of the world was totally wrapped up in legends.

The Blessed Isles

The western extremity was the Blessed Isles. The earliest mention of it, by the Greek poet Hesiod, dates from about 800 B.C. It is clearly related to the Elysium mentioned in

Homer's *Iliad*. The gods, says Hesiod, reward certain individuals by transporting them beyond the Pillars of Hercules, westward to the Islands of the Blessed, where they live in ease and luxury and never die. We know that the Greeks did not pass through the Strait of Gibraltar until about 620 B.C., so it is assumed that this story entered Greek mythology from Phoenician sources.

(More than a thousand years later, Celtic stories repeated this vision of a happy or blessed land beyond the sunset. The Land of Youth, Land of Women, and Plain of Pleasure in Celtic tales all have their Greek counterpart. The Celts came originally from central Europe, but we cannot say for sure that they carried a Greek legend of the Blessed Isles with them. For one thing, the Greek tale was probably derived from outside sources. For another, the Celtic version is apparently more than a borrowed myth. As we know from the Brendan material, it seems to incorporate some real knowledge of the western seas. Actually, the Blessed Isles of the Celts is a land closer to the Norse Vineland than to the legends of Homer and Hesiod.)

The sources of the Blessed Isles are older than either the Celts or the Greeks. They go back to ancient mythic material—journeys over water, ideas about the realm of the dead, and even the natural phenomenon of the sunset.

Water and sunset are part of the earliest myths about the Kingdom of the Dead. The ancient Egyptians believed that the dead were ferried across a still river, the River of Last Things, into the Beyond; the Sumerians had a similar belief. Gilgamesh crosses the waters of death in the famous Sumerian epic named for him. The association of death with a journey by water lasted until Homer's time. Circe tells Odysseus that the realm of the dead lies beyond the great Ocean sea. But even then the concept was changing, and the idea was taking hold that the realm of the dead was below the earth's surface. Odysseus does go underground after crossing the great Ocean.

With the introduction of an underworld, the unknown West became less sinister. In fact, it became more beautiful, for Elysium, the Fields of the Blessed, was situated in the West. In Homer's *Iliad*, Menelaus is told that he will not die, but that the gods will send him to the Elysian plain at the world's end. There life is easy; there no snow or rain falls, and no strong winds blow; there only the West Wind's refreshing breeze blows on everyone. In this passage thousands of years of belief reached poetic expression in a most happy vision. Here is the legendary and literary source of the Blessed Isles that appear in much later poetry.

Meanwhile, there were also nonpoetic references in classical literature to real land to the west. The philosopher Plato believed that "at the edge of the Ocean, lay a great continent," which he said was west of Atlantis. This reference is probably not to a continent in our sense, certainly not to North or South America. It is more likely a reference to the land around the world's Ocean, a girdle of land that kept all the water in place. Aristotle believed that the earth was a sphere and that a single sea extended from the Pillars of Hercules to India. Thus, for Aristotle as for Columbus eighteen centuries later, western shores meant the east coast of Asia.

What was the thinking of Eratosthenes, the scientific geographer? "Only that area of the earth in which we ourselves live and which is known to us," he said, "is called by us *Oikoumene.*" Then he went on to say there may be one or more inhabited continents in the earth's temperate zone. Thus he left the door open for future geographers to add continents to the world map. But he did not actually say he knew of any other continents.

However, two puzzling and intriguing references are

well worth our consideration. One is from Plutarch (A.D. c.46–c.120), the famous Greek biographer. He wrote of an island called Ogygia (not the one from the *Odyssey*), about five days' sail westward from Britannia. Beyond it were other islands, including the one where Zeus imprisoned Cronus, and a "large continent beyond those islands and the sea." From Plutarch's description modern scholars have assumed he was referring to Iceland, Greenland, and North America. But even these scholars admit there is no evidence that the ancients knew of these places firsthand or that they had reached America.

The most intriguing reference comes from the geographer Pausanius, writing about A.D. 150. Far west of the Ocean, he said, lies a group of islands whose inhabitants are red-skinned and whose hair is like that of a horse. Is this what it most obviously sounds like—a reference to American Indians? The scholars cannot agree, and most prefer to consider it a reference to eskimos. Even though it is possible that ancient voyagers to Britain were blown off course to Iceland, or thereabouts, and returned with stories of strange natives, there is much more evidence to support the classical world's knowledge of the far north than of the far west.

The Unseen Southern Continent

Of the four ends of the earth, the southern one was surely the most unusual. *Terra australis incognita,* means the unknown southern land. It was known to be there, even though no one had ever seen it, entirely as a result of classical theorizing.

Greek and Roman geographers believed in the Pythagorean theory of four land masses. Pythagoras, a philosopher and scientist of the sixth century B.C., was greatly concerned with the mathematical relationships of things. According to his theory, the known world of Europe, Asia, and Africa was symmetrically balanced on the globe by three other (unknown) land areas. Pythagoras' ancient notion was revived in Roman times by Crates of Mallos.

Crates believed that the land mass of the known world occupied one quarter of the globe, the northern part of the eastern hemisphere. About 169 B.C., as a contribution to Roman knowledge, he worked out the other three areas as dictated by Pythagorean reasoning. The names he gave to these areas are known to us from an encyclopedia prepared much later, in the fifth century A.D. The people south of the known world were called *antoikoi,* opposite ones. In the northern half of the western hemisphere were the *antipodes,* opposite-footed ones. And in the southern half of the western hemisphere dwelled the *antichthones,* those of the opposite world.

Strangely enough—or presciently—this Pythagorean world devised by Crates presumed two continents in the western hemisphere—centuries before Columbus. On the other hand, the known world of Europe, Asia, and Africa was considered one land mass. Here again was that old misconception that Asia and Africa were joined below the Indian Ocean.

Early travelers reported that a southern continent, which they called Taprobane, existed south of India. Actually they were giving exaggerated reports of Ceylon. When Ptolemy mapped the world in the second century A.D. he made Taprobane (Ceylon) an island; but he extended southeast Africa below it. Even as geographical knowledge improved, such geographical fancies as the southern continent remained fixed in everyone's mind. The Arab geographer Idrisi repeated Ptolemy's misconception and added variations of his own. Knowing the true shape of

Africa's east coast, Idrisi could not have it connect with India. So he moved various of Ptolemy's fictitious features onto the convenient southern continent.

Arab geographers after Idrisi simply stated that the Atlantic and Indian oceans were connected by a narrow channel between Africa and the southern continent. A tenth-century map shows the southern continent separated from Africa by a strip of water. This channel was reportedly full of moving mountains. We recognize in this report a familiar legend related to Jason's clashing rocks.

In time the argument for a southern continent was supported by medieval theology. Besides, no one was anxious to disprove it, because sailing the southern seas was not to be pursued lightly. Aristotle had long ago warned that tropical heat would condense water to the consistency of jelly. Eventually the Portuguese, spurred by Prince Henry, began the slow business of moving down Africa's west coast. By 1487 Bartholomew Díaz reached the "Cape of Storms" at what he said was the tip of Africa. Renamed the "Cape of Good Hope" to encourage sailors, it was rounded ten years later by Vasco da Gama, who landed in India on May 20, 1498.

Meanwhile, Columbus and other voyagers were opening up the western hemisphere. In 1519 Magellan set sail on what would be the first voyage around the world. Passing through the strait at the tip of South America now named for him, Magellan saw a cloud-covered land to his left, that is, farther south. At night it was dotted with fires, and he called it *Tierra del Fuego*, "Land of Fire." Because he did not realize he had merely passed a large island, Magellan strengthened the argument for a southern continent.

Further misconceptions kept the argument alive. Some years after Magellan, Portuguese sailors in the South Pacific were blown off course by a storm east of Borneo. Afterward they reported coming upon an unknown land. Nineteen years later the Spaniards rediscovered this land, calling it New Guinea, because the natives seemed to them like Africans. Such discoveries served to confirm the great southern continent in many people's minds. In 1531 the cartographer Oronce Fine drew a world map on which the continent appeared as *Terra Australis*. Usually it was shown simply as *Terra incognita*. The great cartographer Mercator drew the continent in some detail in his famous 1569 Chart of the World. It was quite an extensive continent, as Mercator drew it. (However, if you know about the Mercator projection—our most familiar kind of world map—you will remember that land areas are "stretched" the nearer they are to the poles.) More to the point, Mercator included Tierra del Fuego as part of the southern continent.

Numerous voyages in the South Pacific, largely by Dutch seamen, did not remove the southern continent from men's minds. Even the eventual discovery of Australia, in the middle of the seventeenth century, did not dispel the notion. And when Abel Janszoon Tasman rounded Australia, *that* did not end the matter. Only after Captain Cook found Antarctica and showed it to be a small continent under an enormous layer of ice did the idea finally perish. The awesome reality of Antarctica was the only argument strong enough to lay to rest the theoretical great southern continent.

The Ends Of The Earth

There are two far places of the ancient world that have other than classical associations. One is Punt, the distant goal of Egyptian captains; the other is Tartessus, the Biblical Tarshish. Both are connected with trade; both were, in their day, synonymous with the ends of the earth. Punt and Tartessus are semilegendary and shrouded in mystery, because the location of one is uncertain and the site of the other has been obliterated from the face of the earth.

The journey to Punt was special enough to warrant particular mention in a mariner's tomb and a pharaoh's temple. The pharaoh was special too, being a woman—Hatshepsut, whom James H. Breasted, the Egyptian scholar, called "the first great lady in world history." She began her reign as pharaoh about 1500 B.C. Her chancellor or prime minister, Senmut, was anxious about having a woman on the throne. He advised her to do something to please the priests and the public, and suggested sending an expedition to Punt, the Land of God.

In 1493 B.C. Hatshepsut sent five galleys of thirty oarsmen each on the journey to Punt. The fleet returned about two years later, and Hatshepsut inscribed an account of the voyage on the temple walls at Dehr el Bahri. "The ships were laden full with the costly products of the Land of Punt," she wrote, and listed valuable woods, resin, frankincense, ebony, ivory, gold, and incense, as well as some native animals and people. Hatshepsut's inscription also mentions "blue stones, green stones and other costly gems," which were probably Indian emeralds, turquoises, lapis lazuli, and sapphires.

We know from other sources that Hatshepsut was actually reviving a voyage of great significance to even earlier Egyptians. Punt was a source of incense, which was widely used in temples, and this made it a very special place. A very expensive item, incense ordinarily came from southern Arabia, and was carried by caravan along special routes to what is now Aden. From there it was carried northward along the Red Sea coast to a point where caravans branched off either to Egypt or to Syria and Babylon. Incense was also obtainable along the east coast of Africa, which may be a clue to the location of Punt.

The first expedition to Punt in search of incense took

OVERLEAF: *The New World according to a 1545 map. The Atlantic coastlines are reasonably accurate, but not the Pacific, reflecting the knowledge acquired from European voyages of discovery.*

Cathay
INDIA ſuperior
Quinſay
Archipelagus 7448 inſularũ
Zipangri
Chamaho
Panuco
Inſ. Tortucarũ
Temiſtitan
Inſ. p̄donum
Catigara
Inſ. infortu natae
Calenſuan
Mare pacificum

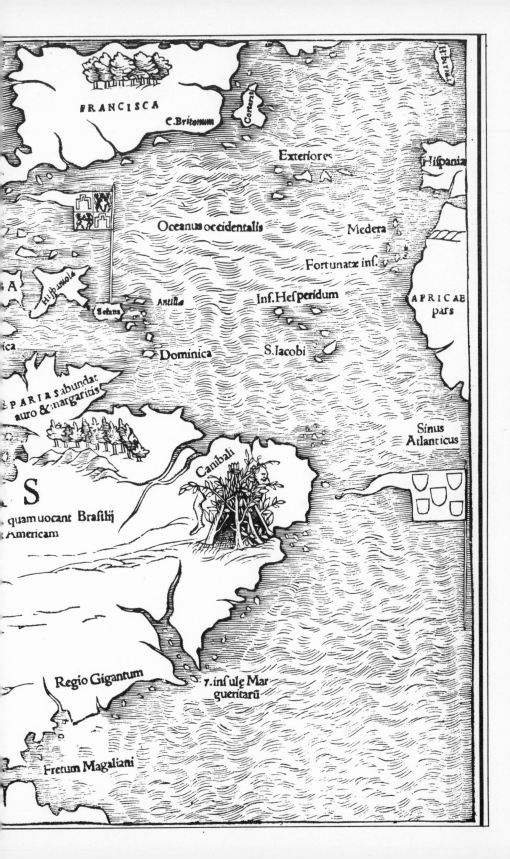

FRANCISCA

C. Britonum

Corterat

Exteriores

Hɪbɪrɪa

Hispania

Oceanus occidentalis

Medera

Fortunatæ inſ.

Inſ. Heſperidum

AFRICAE
pars

Antilla

Hɪſpaniola

Sebana

Dominica

S. Iacobi

Sinus
Atlanticus

ⱯBA

ɪca

EPARIAS abundat
auro & margaritis

S

quam uocant Braſilij
Americam

Canibali

Regio Gigantum

7. inſulę Mar
gueritarū

Fretum Magaliani

place about 3000 B.C.; and similar expeditions continued until about 2300 B.C. We know this from the grave of the Egyptian Knemhotep, who died about 2300 B.C. An inscribed tablet in the grave identifies him as the helmsman to a captain Khui. It also says he journeyed eleven times back and forth to Punt, the Land of God. Sometime in the eight centuries between Knemhotep and Hatshepsut the voyages were discontinued.

Where was Punt? The temple paintings that accompany Hatshepsut's inscription lead scholars to believe that the inhabitants of Punt were Hottentots. This would place Punt in southern Africa. Knemhotep's grave indicates that the Egyptians of his time used antimony as a pigment. The best guess as to their source of this metal is that it came from the area of the Zambesi River, modern Rhodesia. We know that more familiar Egyptian sources of antimony were discovered only much later. But wherever Knemhotep found the antimony, gold was found along with it. The rich source of these precious minerals, it is thought, must have been Punt.

So the clues place Punt in southern Africa, inland from what is now the Mozambique coast. If so, it must have been a busy place even before 2000 B.C. We know that Indian precious stones were brought to Egypt in Hatshepsut's time, along with incense, by way of the Arabian caravan routes. Their presence at Punt seems to confirm that there were early trade routes across the Indian Ocean, between Ceylon and eastern Africa.

If Punt was situated along the Zambesi, the voyage there from Egypt, along the African coast, was about five thousand miles in each direction. This great distance has led some scholars to place Punt at about half the distance. They locate it at Cape Guardafui, where the Gulf of Aden opens into the Indian Ocean. But there is no reason to suppose the Egyptians could not manage the longer voyage. We must not be put off by the fact that later voyages of great length were undertaken only by the Phoenicians. The voyage could have been made in boats no bigger than those used on the Nile. The boats would have to have been stronger than Nile boats, but wood for them was available from the famous cedars of Lebanon. The great importance that Senmut and Hatshepsut placed on the expedition suggests that the longer voyage is the more likely one. And the clues found in Hatshepsut's temple inscription and the wall paintings all support the greater distance.

Fabulous places often exist "far away." Colchis lay at the edge of Jason's world, and the Land of Promise lay at the edge of St. Brendan's. In James Hilton's *Lost Horizon*, a popular novel of the 1930's, the fabulous Shangri-La is situated somewhere in the remoteness of Tibet. And distance is one of the two special features of the Biblical Tarshish.

There are only about a half-dozen references to Tarshish in the Bible. Some just mention its name, others refer to its ships. But, when Jonah tries to flee from the Lord, he boards a ship bound for Tarshish, indicating that it lay at the far side of the Biblical world. A distant city famous for its ships; overly proud of them according to another Biblical reference—what and where was it? We now associate it with a once fabulously wealthy city, Tartessus, in southern Spain.

What made Tartessus important and wealthy was bronze. The discovery of bronze, a mixture of 90 percent copper and 10 percent tin, marked a revolution in prehistoric Europe—the end of the Stone Age. It also created an interest in Britain and Spain, where both copper and tin could be found. About 1500 B.C., when the mines near Tartessus began to give out, the city was important enough and rich enough to survive. It simply switched from mineral production to trade. The ships of Tartessus, as the Bible indicates, were world famous. But Minoan Crete ruled the sea trade at that time. We know that the Minoans sailed to Tartessus and even to Britain because Cretan objects dating from 1700 B.C. have been found in western Britain.

Minoan Crete ruled the Mediterranean, but Tartessus may have found another area for its ships to explore. The Tartessans had probably discovered Madeira and the Canaries by 1500 B.C. There is evidence to suggest that they even reached the west coast of Africa. After the collapse of Minoan Crete control of the sea trade passed to the Phoenicians. The western stronghold of the Phoenicians was Carthage, nine miles north of modern Tunis, on the Mediterranean coast of Africa. About 530 B.C. Carthage conquered Spain and blocked the Strait of Gibraltar. Tartessus' days were numbered.

At that point bronze was being replaced in importance by iron. The trade rivalry between Tartessus and Carthage had to do with something other than bronze. The Phoenicians of Carthage had their eye on the Atlantic islands of Madeira and the Canaries. They were a source of vegetable dyes, and Phoenician dyes were a major item of trade. The Tartessans enjoyed a monopoly in the Atlantic trade, and this was something Carthage meant to stop. In fact, Carthage decided to wipe out Tartessus.

So complete was the destruction of Tartessus that modern excavations have not been able to bring any of it to light. The Phoenicians of Carthage had already established a city of their own in southern Spain, which survives as modern Cádiz. With the fall of Tartessus the Phoenicians monopolized the western seas. They made doubly sure of their control by spreading stories of demons, monsters, and darkness in those waters, and great fields of seaweed from which ships could not free themselves. Two thousand years later Prince Henry's sailors still feared them.

"For a day of the Lord shall come upon all the ships of Tarshish," prophesied Isaiah in the second half of the eighth century B.C. Two hundred years later his prediction came true with a vengeance. All the ships, all the riches, all the pride and power of Tarshish were gone. Of Tartessus, the Biblical Tarshish, not even the stones remain.

PART TWO

Traveling to Neverland

INTRODUCTION 🪶

A LEGEND about a fabulous voyage to a fantastic place represents one kind of journey to Neverland; a modern scientific explanation of the facts behind that legend represents another. Up to now we have looked at various ways in which facts turned into legends. Now we come to four of the most famous Neverlands of all—Atlantis, Camelot, the Kingdom of Prester John, and El Dorado. With the first two in particular we shall see how scientists are turning legends into facts. With the Kingdom of Prester John and El Dorado we come to the end of our journey. We arrive at the ultimate Neverlands: places that never were, though countless people sought them for years. El Dorado was originally the Gilded Man before he gave his name to the place he supposedly ruled. But neither man nor place was real. And Prester John, the great ruler, was probably never more than wishful thinking.

SIX

Lost & Found Atlantis

THE most widely discussed legendary place in the Western world is the lost continent of Atlantis. It was first mentioned more than two thousand years ago, and since then has been the subject of thousands of books, articles, and scholarly arguments. Today there is strong evidence to suggest that the story of Atlantis was based on fact.

One thing separates Atlantis from the true myths of ancient Greece—its origin. The story of Atlantis comes to us fully formed from the Greek philosopher Plato (427–347 B.C.), the most famous of the classical philosophers. He founded a school in Athens known as the Academy, which lasted until A.D. 529, when the Roman emperor Justinian closed it down. Plato's teacher was the philosopher Socrates, and his most famous pupil was Aristotle. Thus the story of Atlantis stems from a man who was central to classical Greek thought.

Plato told the story of Atlantis in two Dialogues, *Timaeus* and *Critias*. (It is important to remember that

Plato. The original and only authentic account of Atlantis appears in two of his Dialogues.

these works represent the only source of the story. Most of the thousands of books and articles on Atlantis were written long after Plato's time—the bulk of them in the last two centuries.)

Plato's Dialogues were discussions by two or more people, one of whom was often Socrates. The people involved in the two discussions of Atlantis are actual historical figures. In addition to Socrates there is Critias, a distant relative of Plato's, at whose house the discussions take place. There are also Timaeus, an astronomer, and Hermocrates, a Syracusan general living in exile in Athens. The date of the discussions is early June of 421 B.C., at which time Plato was actually a small boy. The day is the one following the discussion recorded in *The Republic*, Plato's most famous Dialogue. The actual composition of the two Atlantis Dialogues followed that of *The Republic* by several years. But, because Plato dated them in close sequence some people feel that his Atlantis is simply an extension of the ideal state he discusses in *The Republic.*

Whether or not he was telling of a real place, or of a place he believed to have once been real, Plato gives his story a real source. The tale, he says, was first told to Solon (c.640–c.558 B.C.), the famous Athenian statesman, while he was in Egypt. Solon never wrote the story down in a proper epic poem, but he did tell it to his dear friend Dropides. And Dropides told it to his son Critias, who told it to his grandson, the Critias who figures in Plato's Dialogue.

The story begins with an Egyptian priest who tells Solon of events that took place some nine thousand years earlier. There had been at that time another Athens (which was later destroyed) and a mighty enemy nation threatening to overrun Europe and Asia. This nation came from a distant point in the Atlantic Ocean, beyond the Pillars of Hercules, from a large island named Atlantis. A traveler could pass from Atlantis to smaller islands and from them to the shore of the continent bordering the Western Ocean. The entire area was part of an Atlantean confederation that also ruled over western Europe as far as Italy and over Africa up to Egypt.

The Atlanteans decided to push their conquest farther east and enslave the Athenians, the Egyptians, and the whole Mediterranean world. The gallant warriors of the earlier Athens led a coalition of defenders, and then, when deserted by all their allies, stood alone and defeated the invaders. Soon after there occurred terrible earthquakes and floods. In a single, awful day and a night the Athenian army was swallowed up. Likewise, the whole island of Atlantis was swallowed up and vanished in a day and a night. All that was left was an impassable shoal of mud in that part of the ocean where Atlantis once had been.

That is as much of the Atlantis story as appears in the Dialogue called *Timaeus*. Plato's description of Atlantis itself appears in *Critias*, a Dialogue that he never completed. There he briefly retells the story in *Timaeus* and reminds his audience that the events took place nine thousand years earlier. But, unfortunately, his dating seems to have gotten mixed up. In *Timaeus* he dates the *creation* of the earlier Athens at nine thousand years before the telling of the story. In *Critias* he dates its *destruction* and that of Atlantis at the same time. This inconsistency has troubled some critics of the story, but it may be the result of his not finishing or revising the Dialogue.

The description of Atlantis begins with some mythical history. Plato traces the island back to Poseidon, the sea god. Poseidon raised five sets of twin sons, among whom he divided the rule of the Atlantean confederacy. The eldest son and chief ruler was Atlas, from whom the names of both Atlantis and the Atlantic Ocean are derived. Some people say the Atlas Mountains, across from Gibraltar in North Africa, are also named for him. (The Atlas Mountains, however, are usually associated with the Atlas who holds the earth on his shoulders, another figure entirely.) In any event, a century before Plato, Herodotus called the Western Ocean the Atlantic, and he was apparently the first to do so.

According to Plato, the island of Atlantis was rich in most of the requirements of daily life and was particularly rich in metals. He specifically mentions orichalcum, a precious yellow metal that was once considered second in value only to gold, but which was probably a type of brass. True brass, an alloy of copper and zinc, was unknown to the Greeks. However, cadmia, a crude mixture of metallic oxides, including zinc oxide, was known to them. Whatever orichalcum may have been, it was a legendary substance by Plato's time.

The island was abundantly supplied with timber and a variety of wild and domesticated animals, especially elephants. There were also fountains of cold and hot water, a system of canals and aqueducts, lush fields, and trees of great height and beauty. Palaces, temples, bridges, harbors, docks, and an enormous racetrack graced the island. Many of these were situated in the City of Atlantis on the island's south shore.

The metropolis was uniquely shaped—a series of concentric rings of land and water. At the center was a circular acropolis, crowned by a royal palace and a temple dedicated to Poseidon. Around the acropolis, or citadel, ran a ring of water; then one of land; a second ring of water; still another one of land, containing the racetrack; and a third ring of water. Each of the rings was slightly wider than the preceding one, and the third ring of water was surrounded by a very wide circle of land, girdled by a great wall. The circles of water were crossed by bridges; a canal cut through the rings of land to the open sea. The canal was three hundred feet wide, one hundred feet deep, and several miles long. The waterways were bordered with stone quarried from beneath the central island. Some of this stone was white, some black, and some red. The outermost wall was covered with bronze; an inner wall was covered with tin. The wall around the acropolis was covered with orichalcum that sparkled like fire.

The entire area was heavily populated, and the canal and harbors were filled with ships. The level plain surrounding the city gave way to mountains that were higher and more beautiful than any existing in Plato's time. Fertile meadows, rich villages, rivers, and lakes rounded out the landscape. The happy inhabitants of this fortunate island were blessed with two abundant crops a year. They were a powerful people—their army contained ten thousand chariots, says Plato, and their navy twelve hundred ships. As long as a divine element existed in their nature they remained as virtuous as they were powerful.

Unfortunately, their human nature overcame the divine element, and the Atlanteans became debased. Zeus, in an attempt to punish and thus improve them, summoned all the gods together. "And when he had assembled them," says Plato, "he spoke thus:"—at which point the story of Atlantis comes to an abrupt end. Everything that has been written since has this incomplete, somewhat confusing, at times inconsistent story as its basis.

How the Atlantis Legend Grew

The classical world treated the Atlantis story lightly. Aristotle mentioned Atlantis once, saying: "He who invented it also destroyed it." Pliny also mentioned Atlantis, adding the remark, "if we can believe Plato." And Plutarch referred to "the history or fable of the Atlantic Island." Classical writers seem to have felt that Plato invented Atlantis for philosophical purposes. One classical writer who held a different opinion was Poseidonius (c.135–51 B.C.), a scientist, geographer, astronomer, and historian who lived at Rhodes. A student of earthquakes and other natural forces, he said "it is possible that the story about the island of Atlantis is not a fiction." Poseidonius also believed that men could sail westward from Europe and reach India.

Early Christian writers identified Atlantis with the Biblical Paradise, but the whole subject lay quiet until the age of discovery. A Spanish historian, Francisco López de Gómara (1510–1560), was the first to propose that the American continent was really what Plato had in mind. The idea was repeated by Sir Francis Bacon (1561–1626), the English philosopher-statesman and author of *The New*

Atlantis. The idea that Atlantis was really America was popularized by Janus Joannes Bircherod, a German scholar who proclaimed, in 1663: "the New World is not new."

But did Plato mean that Atlantis was *across* the Atlantic or in the *middle* of the ocean? Athanasius Kircher (1601–1680), the Jesuit scholar, did not believe Plato had America in mind. Kircher, who confused elephant bones with the skeleton of Polyphemus (page 40), wrote a book called *The Subterranean World.* In that work he included a map of Atlantis, placing it in the middle of the Atlantic Ocean.

In 1675 Olaus Rudbeck of Uppsala, Sweden, published *Atlantica*, a book that "proved" Atlantis was really southern Sweden. Ten years later a German, Georg Kaspar Kirchmaier, located Atlantis in South Africa. In 1779 a Frenchman, Jean Sylvain Bailly, said Plato's reference to unnavigable seas pointed to ice floes. He put Atlantis north of Scandinavia, around the island of Spitsbergen. Meanwhile, other scholars were locating it in the Caucasus and on the island of Ceylon. But the Americas were the favored locale, and this led in time to a theory of *two* lost continents—Atlantis and Mu.

The confusion began with Diégo de Landa, a Spanish missionary who became Bishop of Yucatán. He is best known for having destroyed all the available samples of Mayan literature. To make matters worse, he provided his own version of the Mayan alphabet in his book, *Relación de las Cosas de Yucatán.* Scholars later determined that Mayan writing was really ideographic, not alphabetic. Bishop de Landa had produced an "alphabet" of his own invention, although he did, at least, provide a correct explanation of Mayan numerals and the Mayan calendar. The *Relación* was lost until 1864, when it was discovered in a library in Madrid. At this point it entered the Atlantis controversy.

A French scholar, Abbé Brasseur, used the Landa alphabet to translate one of the few Mayan books that had survived—the *Troano Codex*. Brasseur's translation of this rare book included a description of a volcanic eruption. He also found two symbols resembling M and U that he said represented the name of the place destroyed by the volcano. This is the origin of Mu, a lost world of little believability. Modern scholars have shown that Landa's alphabet is gibberish, and that Brasseur's translation is completely wrong. The *Troano Codex* is an astrological work, in no way concerned with volcanic eruptions.

Brasseur's fantasy was kept alive in the late nineteenth century by a French excavator of Mayan ruins in Yucatán. He came upon a series of scenes depicted on the walls of Chichén Itzá. These he interpreted as the story of a lady named Moo. This lady was supposed to be Queen of Atlantis, or Mu. According to the French excavator's version, the lady flees when her continent sinks, changes her name to Isis, builds the Sphinx, and founds Egyptian civilization. (Chichén Itzá, famous for its Mayan ruins, dates from A.D. 530; the Sphinx is thousands of years older.) Edward Herbert Thompson (1860–1935), who began years of archaeological work at Chichén Itzá in 1890, went there in search of Atlantis. Before he began his own excavations at the site he wrote a popular article, "Atlantis Not a Myth," relating the civilization of the Mayas to that of the lost Atlantis civilization.

Interest in Atlantis reached a high point at this time through the writings of Ignatius Donnelly, whose theories will be discussed in detail a little later on. Meanwhile, Mu remained in the picture. In 1912 Paul Schliemann, whose grandfather discovered Troy, made a startling announcement. He said his grandfather had left him objects inscribed in Phoenician "From the King Cronos of Atlantis." And he said he could confirm the existence of a former continent, called Atlantis by the Greeks and Mu by the Mayas. It was a rather obvious hoax, and the inconsistencies in his story were quickly pointed out.

In 1926 "Colonel" James Churchward published *The Lost Continent of Mu,* the first of several books he wrote on the subject. Mu, he said, was a lost continent in the Pacific, the counterpart of Atlantis in the Atlantic. Its location was similar to that of Lemuria, which brings us to still another theory. Geologists in the late nineteenth century proposed the idea that a land bridge once existed between India and Africa. Madagascar, they said, was the surviving remnant of this bridge, which disappeared about sixty million years ago. They called it Lemuria because lemurs, abundant on Madagascar, were similar to primates found in India. Although this oddity seemed to confirm the idea of a land bridge in early geological times, geologists have since abandoned the idea of land bridges in favor of the theory of drifting continents. But other commentators did not abandon Lemuria.

Lemuria and Atlantis were discussed by Mme. Helena P. Blavatsky, (1831–1891) a famous occultist. (Belief in the occult, or supernatural, seems to go hand-in-hand with belief in Lemuria, Mu, and Atlantis. Even Plato's original account of Atlantis has supernatural overtones.) Occultists after Mme. Blavatsky moved Lemuria from the Indian Ocean to the Pacific, relating it to the mysterious statues on Easter Island. If these lost continents attracted mystics and believers in the occult, Atlantis, at least, has also attracted a number of scientific investigators. For example, as early as 1909 in England, and 1921 in the United States, experts suggested that Atlantis was a "poetic memory" of Minoan Crete. This theory was repeated and expanded upon by various scholars.

Conflicting Theories

Plato's account of Atlantis contains references that are vague enough to be interpreted more than one way. Two of the main points of the story that remain open to interpretation are where Atlantis was located and how it was destroyed. Atlantis was said to be in the west, beyond the Pillars of Hercules; this gives us a direction, but not a location. The reference to a continent beyond the Atlantic has been taken to mean America. But is this likely? There is no other reference in all of Plato's writings to a continent or continents beyond the Atlantic, and as we know, there is nothing definite to connect the classical world with America. We cannot be sure that the Phoenicians, the great sea travelers of ancient times, sailed beyond Madeira and the Canary Islands.

If Plato was referring, in a vague way, to Madeira and the Canaries, then the continent beyond could have been the western bulge of Africa. Indeed, if Plato's account reflects Phoenician voyages, the west coast of Africa seems most likely as the location for the far continent. A voyage out into the Atlantic and down to the African coast is historically possible, even probable. The shoals west of the Pillars of Hercules, mentioned by Plato, may have been invented by the Phoenicians to discourage others from voyaging in *their* waters.

Examining the matter further we come to another theory. Is there a connection between Atlantis and the legendary city of Tartessus? It has been suggested that the "shoals" are actually an ambiguous reference to the silting up of the Guadalquivir River in Spain, one of the presumed sites of lost Tartessus. A relationship between two lost civilizations fascinates some observers.

The location of Atlantis at the western edge of Phoenician power can be supported by odd bits of information. For instance, Plato speaks of elephants in Atlantis. Elephants of a now extinct subspecies used to roam Morocco in northwestern Africa, which can be made to "fit" as the western continent. There are also some curious relationships: Theorists point out that Atlantis resembles Homer's Scheria, the land of the Phaeacians in the *Odyssey*—and both Atlantis and Scheria resemble what we have been told about Tartessus.

Although we don't know with certainty that Plato knew of the Phoenician's voyages, we can definitely settle another argument—that Atlantis was a mid-Atlantic continent. Modern techniques in geology and oceanography have established that the ocean floor is millions of years old, much older than human life on our planet. Even the youngest volcanic outcroppings rising from the ocean floor date from long before the rise of any civilization. Plato's text has been interpreted to mean either that there was a continent *across* the Atlantic or a continent out *in* the Atlantic. But science has eliminated the possibility of a mid-Atlantic continent that either appeared or disappeared within any human memory.

The other point open to interpretation is how Atlantis was destroyed. What was the catastrophe to which Plato referred? A volcanic eruption cannot cause an entire continent to sink, nor can an earthquake swallow up or crumble an entire civilization. And yet Plato's account specifies a combination earthquake and flood. We know that Plato was familiar with earthquakes because the historian Thucydides described a *tsunami*, a wave accompanying an earthquake, which occurred when Plato was an infant. Did Plato read this description? We don't know; but an earthquake and accompanying tsunami, with or without volcanic action, is consistent with nature and with Plato's story.

One of the things that makes it hard to believe in Atlantis is that Plato dated its destruction nine thousand years before Solon. No human civilization has been found that is that old, though primitive societies did exist even earlier. But the idea that an advanced civilization flourished eleven thousand, five hundred years ago constitutes a stumbling block for some people. Another problem is the absence of any mention of Atlantis outside of Plato's writings. No earlier Greek writer mentioned it, and it does not appear in the literature of other early cultures. To some people this means that Atlantis can only be Plato's invention.

Ignatius Donnelly's Popular Theory

Ignatius Donnelly (1831–1901) was a Pennsylvania lawyer who moved to Minnesota and entered politics in the mid-nineteenth century. He was elected lieutenant governor at the age of twenty-eight, served two terms in Congress, and helped found the Populist Party. In his later years he became an enormously popular writer. His science fiction novel, *Caesar's Column*, sold a million copies. Another one of his popular books, *The Great Cryptogram*, attempted to prove that Bacon wrote Shakespeare's plays. His most famous book is *Atlantis: The Antediluvian World*. It has gone through more than fifty printings since its first appearance in 1882, and is still available and still popular.

The term *antediluvian* means very old or primitive, but refers specifically to the time before the Deluge, Noah's Flood. In 1882, while the followers of Darwin and Lyell were hotly arguing their evolutionary and geological theories with people who believed in a literal reading of the Bible, ancient civilizations were being uncovered and examined amid great public interest and excitement. Donnelly links ancient civilizations, both eastern and western, with Atlantis, but his arguments rest on his misreading of incomplete information. A reader who does not recognize this drawback could find Donnelly's book very convincing.

Donnelly's positive and forceful statements brush aside facts that don't suit his arguments. The book can be summarized in the thirteen points Donnelly says it will demonstrate: (1) "That there once existed in the Atlantic Ocean, opposite the mouth of the Mediterranean Sea, a large island, which was the remnant of an Atlantic continent, and known to the ancient world as Atlantis"; (2) That the description in Plato is not a fable, "but veritable history"; (3) That Atlantis is the place where man rose from barbarism to civilization; (4) That it grew to "a populous and mighty nation," and its people settled the shores of the Gulf of Mexico, the Mississippi, the Amazon, the west coast of South America, the Mediterranean, the west coasts of Europe and Africa, and the Baltic, Black, and Caspian Seas; (5) "That it was the true Antediluvian world"—the Garden of Eden and other paradises—"a universal memory of a great land, where early mankind dwelt for ages in peace and happiness"; (6) That the ancient Greek, Phoenician, Hindu, and Scandinavian gods were simply the kings, queens, and heroes of Atlantis; and that mythology is "a confused recollection of real historical events"; (7) That the mythology of Egypt and Peru was originally the religion of Atlantis: sun worship; (8) That Egypt is probably the oldest colony of Atlantis and was a reproduction of Atlantean civilization; (9) That the implements of Bronze Age Europe came from Atlantis, where iron was also first manufactured; (10) That the Phoenician alphabet came from Atlantis, and the Mayas also received the Atlantean "mother" alphabet; (11) That Atlantis was the seat of the Aryan or Indo-European family of nations, also the Semites and possibly the Tauranian races; (12) That Atlantis "perished in a terrible convulsion of nature," in which the whole island and most of its inhabitants were submerged; (13) That some people escaped and told of the catastrophe. The tale of the destruction of Atlantis survives as "the Flood and Deluge legends of the different nations of the Old and New Worlds."

Donnelly does not believe Atlantis is a Utopian creation based on Plato's own *Republic*. And he finds "nothing improbable" in Plato's description. "It is a plain and reasonable history of a people who built temples, ships, and canals; who lived by agriculture and commerce; who, in pursuit of trade, reached out to all the countries around them". But then he moves on to scientific matters and interprets geological evidence to demonstrate that "such an island must have existed" where Plato located it. He uses geology to show that it is possible for Atlantis to have been destroyed in a night and a day. Unfortunately, he misread his geology, much of which has since been disproven.

Donnelly calls the Azores "the mountain peaks of this drowned island," which he says was a thousand miles wide and two thousand or even three thousand miles long. Modern core samples taken off the Azores show the region to be younger than the main Atlantic floor, but many thousands of years older than any civilization. "Proofs are abundant," says Donnelly, "that there must have been at one time uninterrupted land communication between Europe and America." Then he proceeds to "prove" the land-bridge theory that was open to debate in his own day but which has since been demolished by the theory of continental drift.

One of his principal methods of arguing is to ask questions and then supply the answers. He asks if the memory of so gigantic a catastrophe as the destruction of Atlantis is preserved in mankind's traditions. And he answers himself

A map of Atlantis and mid-Atlantic ridges, according to Ignatius Donnelly's geological theory, which has been disproved.

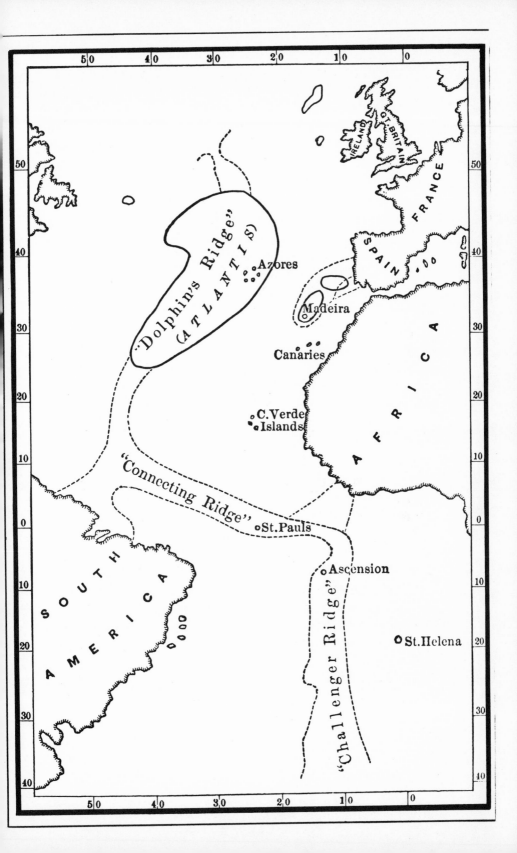

by saying that such a catastrophe "could not fail to impress with terrible force the minds of men, and to project its gloomy shadow over all human history." Then he turns to a number of early cultures of the Old and New Worlds and concludes that "we find everywhere traditions of the Deluge." For him they all "point unmistakably to the destruction of Atlantis."

His strongest arguments (or assumptions) occur where there is an absence of evidence to support them. "If our knowledge of Atlantis was more thorough," he states, "it would no doubt appear that, in every instance wherein the people of Europe accord with the people of America, they were both in accord with the people of Atlantis; and that Atlantis was the common center from which both peoples derived their arts, sciences, customs, and opinions." To support this argument with "evidence," Donnelly poses questions for which there are no satisfactory answers. He then provides his own answers, which always assume the earlier existence of Atlantis. For example: "On the monuments of Central America there are representations of bearded men. How could the beardless American Indians have imagined a bearded race?" To which Donnelly answers, "Atlantis." Another answer sometimes given is that the Phoenicians reached America a few thousand years ago. The technique of asking unanswerable questions works for a great many theories.

The book ends with high praise for the lost civilization of Atlantis. "They were," says Donnelly, "the founders of nearly all our arts and sciences; they were the parents of our fundamental beliefs; they were the first civilizers, the first navigators, the first merchants, the first colonizers of the earth. . . ." This is more than can be said for any civilization in the history books.

One highly developed civilization of the ancient world

was not in the history books when Donnelly wrote about Atlantis. It was not until 1900 that Sir Arthur Evans began digging in Crete—uncovering the magnificent Minoan civilization. Since Donnelly knew nothing of the Minoans, whom modern theorists link with Atlantis, we can only guess at how he might have responded to the modern Minoan theory of Atlantis. He was convinced the lost Atlantis existed out in the Atlantic Ocean, and probably would have scoffed at the idea of its being in the Aegean Sea. Oddly enough, the modern theorists echo some of his arguments. Yet Donnelly mentions the same volcanic eruption that forms the basis of the modern theory linking Atlantis with the Minoans.

A Modern Atlantis Theory

Like Ignatius Donnelly, Plato knew practically nothing about the Minoans, and he lived two thousand years closer to their time. This fact is important to keep in mind as we examine the theory of Professor Anghelos Galanopoulos, a contemporary Greek seismologist who associates Atlantis with a Minoan civilization on the island of Thera. The Minoans, who reached a high level of civilization and produced a rich and mighty culture, were a major power in the ancient world. And yet, by Plato's time they were less than a memory.

The Minoans, of the Mediterranean island of Crete, spread their civilization to mainland Greece and throughout the Aegean Sea, settling such Aegean islands as the Cyclades group, one of which is Thera. Also known as Santorini, it is a volcanic island, with records of volcanic activity dating back to 197 B.C. Eruptions were noted about once every fifty years, and even more frequently in this century. We know, from geological evidence, of two gigantic eruptions on Thera. One took place at least twenty-five thousand years ago, and the other about 1500 B.C. The second eruption has been linked to the sudden decline of Minoan civilization. Professor Galanopoulos also links it to the destruction of Atlantis.

His theory is built upon two specific items in Plato's account: that Atlantis was destroyed in a night and a day; and that the event took place nine thousand years before Solon's time. In addition, Galanopoulos questions the measurements Plato gives in his description of Atlantis and what he considers an error in transcribing the story. Together these elements have led the Greek scientist to an ingenious "discovery" of Atlantis in Minoan waters far from the Atlantic.

Professor Galanopoulos relates Plato's "royal state" and the smaller "metropolis" of Atlantis to the islands of Crete and Thera. He says that Thera was once a populous Minoan center, whose city and palace corresponded to Plato's description of the Atlantean metropolis. We cannot find this city because it was totally destroyed in the gigantic volcanic blast of 1500 B.C. The center of the island disappeared completely, leaving the present crescent shape and a *caldera* thirteen hundred feet deep. (A *caldera*, literally, is a pot, as in the word *cauldron*, a hollowed-out area filled by the sea. When the molten lava under Thera's volcano spewed out it left a vast underground hollow. What remained of the volcano fell into this space. The result was the caldera, or collapsed volcano, that exists today.)

If he could measure the extent of the 1500 B.C. eruption, Professor Galanopoulos decided, he would find a "proof" of his theory. Meanwhile he turned to other measurements. Plato gives the size of the plain in the center of Atlantis as three thousand stadia by two thousand stadia, or approximately three hundred forty by two hundred thirty miles. Galanopoulos came to feel that all measurements given by Plato in the thousands were implausible, but all those in smaller figures were reasonable. In fact, he saw a tenfold error in all figures over a thousand. If this error applied to time as well as distance, then the destruction of Atlantis took place nine hundred—not nine thousand— years before Solon. This would place it at about the time of the Thera eruption.

If the great plain is reduced by a factor of ten, it fits into the plain of Mesara in central Crete. And Crete, says Galanopoulos, was Atlantis' royal state. Moreover, the dimensions of the metropolis, when reduced tenfold, fit into Thera. How can such a tenfold error be accounted for? Professor Galanopoulos says it occurred when the story was transcribed by the Egyptian priests who later repeated it to Solon. An examination of the number system used in Minoan times suggests that such an error is easily possible.

Plato, misled by the tenfold error, put Atlantis out in the ocean, beyond the Pillars of Hercules. But, says Professor Galanopoulos, Hercules' labors were largely performed around Greece. He believes that the Pillars of Hercules refers to a Greek cape, not Gibraltar. He also notes that the geological evidence has disproved the notion of an Atlantic continent. Dating of the mid-Atlantic ridge near the Azores indicates no sunken islands in the last seventy-two thousand years.

Galanopoulos has read the geological evidence differently from Donnelly, but in one point he agrees with him: The eruption at Thera, he says, would have been a major disaster. It would have killed hundreds of thousands of people, washing away many coastal cities in Greece, Turkey, and Crete. It would have set off terrible storms, enormous waves, and a rain of ashes. It would have rocked inland cities and tumbled palaces, turned seas to mud, and day to night. In short, it would have left an impact upon folk memory among all the peoples of a vast area. This folk memory is retained in the story of the destruction of Atlantis.

There, in brief summary, is the theory. What of the proof? In recent years some remarkable discoveries have come to light on Thera, some of which confirm many points of the theory, particularly the connection to Minoan civilization. There had been some excavation on Thera in the nineteenth century, before Evans' work in Crete, but the discovery of Minoan relics meant little at the time. For over a century, however, most of the digging on Thera has been commercial, not archaeological. The island is covered with volcanic ash, which has been mined extensively for the making of cement. There is no way of knowing how many relics were destroyed during this process, compared to the few that were preserved. Only since 1967 has Thera been preserved for archaeological excavation.

In July, 1965, Professor Galanopoulos explained his theory to James W. Mavor, Jr., an American engineer working on deep sea research submarines. Mavor, who decided to conduct underwater research at Thera to prove the professor's theory, organized an expedition for the summer of 1966 that included various experts, among them an archaeologist. Here, at last, was a modern scientific team assembled for the purpose of finding Atlantis. Mavor and his group examined the Thera caldera and surrounding land area using various modern devices, particularly acoustic sounding devices for finding hidden ruins. More important, Mavor had gotten the Research Vessel *Chain*, of Woods Hole Oceanographic Institution, to include Thera as part of its 1966 tour of the Mediterranean. The results of the first season at Thera made headlines around the world. *The New York Times*, on September 4, 1966, announced:

MOAT BELIEVED TO BE PART OF ATLANTIS IS
FOUND IN AEGEAN SEA.

Although the actual findings were not spectacular,
they were archaeologically important. The Greek government was concerned that this major Minoan site would be
overrun by people more interested in "discovering" Atlantis than in protecting the Minoan site. When Mavor
mounted another Thera expedition in the summer of 1967,
he was joined by Spyridon Marinatos, a prominent archaeologist and later Inspector General of Greek Antiquities.
Marinatos became annoyed that Mavor's party was princi-
pally interested in finding clues to Atlantis. After 1967 the
Greek government barred non-Greeks from digging on
Thera. Marinatos was impressed by the Minoan findings
on Thera and felt it was more important to concentrate on
them than on demonstrating the island's possible connection with Atlantis. And yet, the Minoan discoveries only
serve to strengthen Galanopoulos' theory.

How much of the theory did Mavor's expeditions actually prove? Enough, says Mavor, definitely to establish
Thera as lost Atlantis. First of all, his team, aided by the
Chain, confirmed that the 1500 B.C. eruption was enormous. It was, in fact, five times greater than the eruption of
Krakatoa in 1883, which would make it the greatest single
natural disaster witnessed by man.

When Krakatoa erupted, the roar was heard two thousand miles away. Vibrations in the atmosphere broke windows and cracked walls a hundred and fifty miles away; day
turned into night for twenty-four hours in an area two
hundred miles around; and ash was airborne for as far as a
thousand miles. The eruption of Thera was five times as
tremendous. Ash must have fallen all over the Near East. In
1948 a Swedish research team in the Mediterranean examined core samples from the sea floor. One hundred miles

southeast of Thera they found an ash layer traceable to the 1500 B.C. eruption. It was seven feet thick.

The blast left the remnants of three islands—Thera, Therasia and Aspronisi—arranged concentrically around the thirteen hundred-foot-deep caldera. A hole is all that remained of countless cubic miles of earth, lava, ash, and pumice. "This enormous hole," says Mavor, "is the most imposing marine caldera, or collapsed volcano, in the world." Enormous sea waves created by the collapse were pushed by air waves from the blast and became tremendous tsunamis that could have swept over the entire island of Crete. These waves radiated in all directions—to Africa, Asia Minor, and mainland Greece. Even Spyridon Marinatos, as early as 1939, said: "I think there is little reason to doubt that the devastation of the coast sites of Minoan Crete was caused by the waves from the eruptions of Thera." Substitute "Atlantis" for "Minoan Crete" and Plato's story looks less like fable and more like fact.

Galanopoulos placed a drawing of the Atlantean metropolis over a map of Thera drawn to the same scale. It fit perfectly; but some observers are not satisfied with this proof. Mavor believes he has confirmed Galanopoulos' theory. He says we cannot take Plato's harbor scheme literally because the tides in the Aegean would not drain and refresh it. Mavor believes, instead, that there were rambling waterways surrounding ancient Thera's volcanic cones which were converted by Plato's orderly Greek mind into concentric rings of water. As a result of the *Chain*'s seismic readings, Mavor found "a correlation between Thera and the metropolis of Atlantis." The probable land and water layout of Minoan Thera "coincided" with Plato's geometric arrangement.

What makes one kind of evidence more reasonable than another? If we can discredit Donnelly's theory on geological grounds, while Galanopoulos' geology is sound, how much further do we go? What evidence is there of a tenfold error in transcribing numbers over a thousand? The scientific writer Willy Ley considered Galanopoulos' superimposed map a poor fit. He called the similarity in size "just a coincidence." He did not think Thera was Atlantis. But he agreed that the Thera eruption "was the main cause of the Atlantis story."

Perhaps no single theory will answer all the questions about Atlantis. The Greeks, since 1967, have been more interested in Minoan finds on Thera than in "proofs" that it was Atlantis. Mavor was disappointed about giving up the search before more convincing proof could be discovered. As he has said: "It remained to excavate Thera further. . . ." Excavations are continuing on Thera, but for archaeological purposes. Who knows what may be found there someday?

SEVEN

King Arthur's Britain

WHO has not heard of King Arthur and his noble Knights of the Round Table? They are folk heroes, semilegendary figures and familiar literary characters; the Arthurian stories are the national epics of England and Wales. Today we dress them in medieval armor and move them across a vaguely twelfth or thirteenth-century landscape. This is a mistaken notion that has been supported by book illustrators and movie producers who know that the armor, castles, and other trappings of A.D. 1200 make good illustrations and movie scenes. Yet it is to the year 500, approximately, that Arthur belongs.

That last statement implies that there really was a King Arthur. Current scholarship supports the statement, though the real Arthur was nothing like the familiar storybook figure. Archaeologists today are digging for the remains of Camelot and other sites associated with King Arthur. Today we can deal factually with King Arthur's Britain. But before we follow the archaeologists and scholars as they piece together the evidence of Arthurian Britain, we should examine the Arthurian legend. Using historical writings, poems, and stories we can trace the references to Arthur to see how he developed into the familiar figure we know. Once we understand how the legend came to be, we can see how the facts support the legend.

When the Roman legions left Britain, about A.D. 410, after nearly four centuries of occupation, the Roman Empire was crumbling. The Gaels, who had been in Britain for a thousand years, but who had been driven into the hills and mountains of Scotland and Wales, swept down on the cities of Roman Britain. Raiding and burning, they virtually destroyed all of Roman civilization in Britain. By the middle of the fifth century, except for some roads and walls—which remain today—Roman Britain was gone.

At the same time the Angles and Saxons began their coastal raids. At first they returned to their homes in Denmark and northern Germany. Eventually they settled with their families along the rivers and harbors of Britain's east coast. The Angles settled to the north, and Saxons to the south. Other invaders, the Jutes, settled in the extreme southeast, in what is now Kent. By 600 the Gaels had been crushed, enslaved or driven back into the mountains of Wales and Scotland.

The conquests of the fifth and sixth centuries have been recorded in the *Anglo-Saxon Chronicle*, a document compiled in the ninth century, reportedly by order of Alfred the Great. What interests us is that there is a gap in its account of conquests which covers the years we now associate with Arthur's activities. However, church records and histories prepared by churchmen do offer us some information about those years.

One such church historian is Gildas, whose dates (516–570) are not certain; he was probably a contemporary of the real Arthur. This Breton monk, known as Saint Gildas the Wise, is most famous for *De Excidio Britanniae*, or *The Destruction* (or *Loss*) *and Conquest of Britain*, written about 540. A history of Britain from earliest times to Gildas' day, it survived for a thousand years and was printed in 1525. Gildas tells how the Romano-Britons were harrassed by a local ruler, Vortigern. These survivors of Roman civilization in Britain, to keep from being destroyed, "took arms under the conduct of Ambrosius Aurelianus." Gildas calls this "modest man" the last of the Romans. "After this," says Gildas, "sometimes our countrymen, sometimes the enemy, won the field, . . . until the year of the siege of Bath-Hill (Mons Badonicus) when took place also the last almost, though not the least slaughter of our cruel foes."

This great battle, usually referred to as that of Mount Badon, took place forty-four years and one month after the landing of the Saxons. Gildas notes that it was the year of his birth, and scholars have placed it around the year 500. Although Gildas does not name the British leader at Mount Badon, nor does *De Excidio Britanniae* mention Arthur, this account of the battle at Badon is the basis for believing that Arthur really existed.

Another church scholar and Anglo-Saxon historian is the Venerable Bede (673–735). Well versed in many fields, he is credited with starting the custom of fixing dates "A.D.," from the birth of Christ. His great work, the *Ecclesiastical History of the English People*, completed in 731, names the kings of the Britons, but there is no mention of Arthur. However, Bede, who copied a great deal from Gildas, dates Ambrosius Aurelianus at 466 and the battle at Badon at about 493. Like Gildas, he leads us to believe there was a Romano-British leader immediately following Ambrosius.

Sometime between the years 800 and 830 a Welsh monk named Nennius compiled a *Historia Britonum.* This *History of the Britons,* pieced together from Gildas, Bede, and other sources—including oral accounts—provides the first mention of Arthur by name. The book is a mixture of facts, legends, and stories of marvels and miracles. Some people have said that Nennius was invented in the twelfth century by Geoffrey of Monmouth, who quotes the monk in his own history. But modern scholars now accept Nennius' *Historia,* even though the oldest known copy dates from two centuries after his time. Scholars cannot, however, say where Nennius got his material on Arthur.

What is this material? Writing about the son of the first Saxon invader, Nennius says: "Then it was that Arthur was wont to fight against them in those days along with the kings of the Britons, but he himself was *dux bellorum,* leader of battles." Nennius also names twelve battles that Arthur fought. The first was at the mouth of the Gleni River, the next four were at the Dubglas River, and the sixth was on the Bassas River. The seventh was fought in the Wood of Celidon ("Cat Coit Celidon"), and the eighth at Castellum Guinnion, where Arthur carried an image of the Virgin Mary on his shoulders. The ninth was fought at the City of the Legion, the tenth on the Trebuit River, and the eleventh on Mt. Agned. "The twelfth was the battle on Mount Badon, in which there fell together in one day 960 men in one onset of Arthur, and no one laid them low save himself alone. In all the battles he remained victor."

There, in one sentence followed by a brief account of his triumphs, is the first mention by name of Britain's legendary hero. The title *dux bellorum* is probably Roman in origin, though its exact significance is not certain. In the tenth century a chronology, *Annales Cambriae,* was added to Nennius' history. This addition mentions two battles fought by Arthur; one in which he carries a cross for three days and nights, is merely Badon mentioned again. The other, "the action of Camlann, in which Arthur and Medrault fell," is his mysterious last battle. This chronology dates Badon at 516 and Camlann at 537.

William of Malmesbury (1095?–1142?) was an English historian and librarian who is responsible for confusing later commentators. His *Chronicle* (or *Acts*) *of the Kings of England*, written in 1128, repeats the story of Arthur's triumph at Badon. When the Britons were exhausted and their hopes were fading, says William, "they would have come to an end then and there had not Ambrosius the last of the Romans, who was king after Vortigern, harried the hordes of the barbarians through the glorious work of the warrior Arthur." So William mentions Arthur and, like his predecessors, separates him from Ambrosius. But he confuses the dating by making Arthur one of Ambrosius' warriors.

William's final note about Arthur is annoying to some historians. "This," he says, "is that Arthur about whom we hear so much nonsense from British sources nowadays. And yet he deserves the fame which only true history can bestow, instead of the dreams of unreliable legends; for he saved his countrymen from collapse for many years, and roused their courage to endurance and to war." A real man, then, but a source of "much nonsense." What was William suggesting that he did not tell? We do not know; and when Arthur next appears, in Geoffrey of Monmouth's colorful history, he is almost pure legend.

The Legend Begins to Take Shape

Geoffrey of Monmouth, who completed his *History of the Kings of Britain* between 1136 and 1138, reshaped the Arthur story, enlarging his biography and fixing the sequence of events. It was Geoffrey who created the heroic king and introduced, among others, an important character: the wizard Merlin.

Geoffrey, who was also a churchman, was born in Wales about 1100. He spent much of his life at Oxford, but said he used Welsh sources in compiling his history. The history was written because Geoffrey could find nothing outside of Gildas and Bede about "the kings who lived here before the Incarnation of Christ" or about Arthur. "Yet the deeds of these men were such that they deserve to be praised for all time." His contemporaries were skeptical about Geoffrey's *History* and spoke of his "inordinate love of lying." Moreover, they disliked his trying to please the Britons, who had been conquered by the early Saxons; the Norman rulers of Geoffrey's Britain had in turn won the land from the Anglo-Saxons. Geoffrey's creation of an early British hero, so far removed from the Norman-French conquerors, did not please some of his contemporaries. But the majority of his countrymen—not just Welshmen, but the emerging mixed breed who thought of themselves as Englishmen—welcomed such a hero.

In the different versions of Geoffrey's manuscript names change, but the basic story remains the same. It begins with three sons of king Constantine: Constans, Aurelius Ambrosius, and Uther. The Welsh king Vortigern kills Constans, and Aurelius and Uther flee to Brittany. When Vortigern invites the Saxons into Britain, the Britons rebel against him and the Saxons. Vortigern flees to Wales. Enter Merlin, who prophesies Vortigern's overthrow by Aurelius and Uther. They conveniently arrive and Aurelius Ambrosius burns Vortigern in his castle.

Next Aurelius Ambrosius defeats the Saxons in a major battle. He decides to build a memorial in honor of his victory and his fallen comrades. Merlin helps him by magically transporting from Ireland a set of enormous stones

A seventeenth-century picture of King Arthur and his knights. The style of armor is closer to the artist's time than to Arthur's, and the Round Table is shaped like a doughnut.

known as the Giant's Dance. This is Geoffrey's explanation of the building of Stonehenge, an explanation as false as it is fanciful. When Aurelius is treacherously poisoned, he is buried at this "Sepulcher of Stones."

Uther succeeds him as ruler of the Britons. With Merlin's magical assistance, Uther seduces a lady named Igerna, at her castle, Tintagel. The result, in due time, is that she gives birth to Arthur; later, Uther marries Igerna, which is nice for Arthur. When Uther dies, Arthur is crowned king at the age of fifteen. He is a good warrior king who defeats the Saxons in various battles, and his greatest triumph occurs at Bath Hill. Later he goes on to conquer much of Europe.

Toward the end of his career Arthur returns to the continent, leaving his nephew, Mordred, and his queen, Guinevere, to rule Britain in his absence. At Mont St. Michel he battles a giant in an episode that is similar to Odysseus' meeting with Polyphemus. But Arthur is recalled to Britain by news of Mordred's treachery. He fights several battles with Mordred, the last one in Cornwall on the Cambula River. Arthur kills Mordred, but is himself mortally wounded and carried off to the Isle of Avalon.

Geoffrey's work established both the basic story and the theme of chivalry that runs through all later versions. When Arthur holds court at Caerleon there are church services, feasts, and games. "The knights," says Geoffrey, "planned an imitation battle and competed together on horseback, while their womenfolk watched from the top of the city walls and aroused them to passionate excitement by their flirtatious behavior." Here is the origin of the familiar Arthurian scene of children's books and movies. After Geoffrey, Arthur and his knights are no longer Romano-British warriors of the fifth century. They don the armor of medieval times and become chivalric heroes, knights who battle for a lady's favor.

By the middle of the thirteenth century European courts were acting out Arthurian pageants, and continental storytellers added the Round Table and the episode of the sword in the stone to the original material. In the thirteenth century the poet Jean Bodel of Arras told of three themes worth a good storyteller's attention. One was the Matter of the Ancient World: Troy, Aeneas, Alexander the

Great, and the Emperor Constantine, and all the stories woven around them; another was the Matter of France: stories of Charlemagne and his knights, such as Roland; the third was the Matter of Britain: the exploits of King Arthur and the Knights of the Round Table.

The Popular Arthurian Legend

Geoffrey is only one source of the Arthurian material as we know it today. From very early times, probably before the sixth century, Welsh bards orally transmitted history, myths and stories in order to keep the deeds of Welshmen alive. They also felt free to add tall tales and other folk material to their oral histories. By the twelfth century their stories were being written down. Many of them were gathered and translated into English in the nineteenth century in a collection called the *Mabinogion*. These storytellers were Celts, who inhabited Wales, Scotland, Ireland, Brittany (in France), and Cornwall in the west of England, which was Arthur's home territory. Naturally, Arthur became a familiar figure in Celtic tales.

In early Celtic versions of the Arthur story his principal knight was his nephew, Gwalchmei. In English this name becomes Gawain; and Gawain remained a popular hero into the late fourteenth century. (*Sir Gawain and the Green Knight*, one of the best known works of the Middle English period, dates from about 1370.) Kei, or Cei, of the Celtic stories became Sir Kay in English, and Bedwyr became Sir Bedivere. In time, characters and incidents from other story cycles were woven into the Arthurian legend. The story of Tristan and Iseult, a popular romance from Cornwall with a basis in fact, was incorporated into the Arthurian cycle after Geoffrey's time. By then the legend of Arthur was changing to suit the chivalric additions. Arthur had become older, the noble head of a medieval court, and the knights were taking over.

The Celtic Gawain was replaced as chief knight by Lancelot, who first appeared about 1168 in a work by the poet Chrétien de Troyes, and who represents the main French addition to the Arthur story. In later versions of the story, Lancelot's love for Guinevere, and Gawain's disapproval of him, destroy the fellowship of knights at the time of Mordred's betrayal. The Lancelot-Gawain rivalry reflects the mixture of native and continental elements in the story. A French poet, Wace, added the Round Table, and another, Robert de Boron, added the story of the sword in the stone. The Tristan story was Celtic, and Layamon, a native English priest, added the episode of the Isle of Avalon at the end of the story. The Holy Grail, though it appeared in continental poems, probably entered the story from Celtic sources. Some items introduced into the story by Chrétien de Troyes, the Frenchman, were borrowed from Welsh tales. Other material came from ballads and Welsh and Breton popular songs. Finally, in the fifteenth century, all this material was worked into one literary unit by Malory.

With Sir Thomas Malory (1394?–1471) the Arthur legend takes its reasonably final form. His *Morte d'Arthur*, completed in 1469 or 1470, was printed in 1485 by William Caxton, the first English printer. The work is a full compilation of the English and French romances on the subject. It remains the basis of all later versions of the Arthurian material. In Caxton's edition it became extremely popular: There were four separate editions printed in the first hundred years. Our image of King Arthur and the Knights of the Round Table is derived from Malory, including the elements of enchantment, love, loyalty, revenge, and chivalry, and our pictures of Arthur, Guinevere, Merlin, Lancelot, Gawain, Percival, Galahad, and Mordred.

Malory is a mysterious figure. He was apparently a soldier in the Hundred Years' War and a Member of Parliament in 1445. In 1451 he is said to have raided a monastery situated on land that once belonged to him. In any event, he was charged with numerous crimes and imprisoned for the rest of his life. Little else is known about him with any certainty, except that he wrote the *Morte d'Arthur* in prison. The book is a major accomplishment. Malory gave unity to many dissimilar elements by taking native stories, surviving in local dialects, and courtly, sophisticated French romances, and weaving them into one of the great prose works of fifteenth-century English literature.

Shakespeare wrote plays about earlier and later kings, but avoided Arthur. John Milton abandoned an Arthurian theme and turned to *Paradise Lost*. Except for an opera by Dryden, with music by Purcell, the Matter of Britain was largely ignored until Tennyson revived it in the nineteenth century. But it has remained a popular literary subject. The best known modern Arthurian work is T.H. White's four-part novel, *The Once and Future King*. Its first part, *The Sword in the Stone*, was animated by Walt Disney, and the whole work inspired the musical play *Camelot*.

The title of White's novel reflects the Celtic air of mystery surrounding the passing of Arthur. The Welsh believe he was taken to Avalon, a mysterious land in the West, and that he did not really die but will come again. Malory, in line with this belief, called Arthur "rex quondam rexque futuris"—the once and future King.

The Search for Camelot

So much for legend and literature. What are the evidences of a real Arthur? We find them in place names, sites, and objects that have Arthurian connections. Though some of

¶Here foloweth the fyxth boke of the noble and wozthy pzynce kyng Arthur.

¶How fyz Launcelot and fyz Lyonell departed fro the courte foz to feke auentures / ⁊ how fyz Lyonell lefte fyz Laūcelot flepynge ⁊ was taken. Capim.j.

None after that the noble ⁊ wozthy kyng Arthur was comen fro Rome into Englande / all the knyghtes of the roūde table refozted vnto ⁊ kyng and made many iuftes and turneymentes / ⁊ fome there were that were good knyghtes / whiche encreafed fo in armes and wozfhyp that they paffed all theyz felowes in pzoweffe ⁊ noble dedes ⁊ that was well pzoued on many. But in efpecyall it was pzoued on fyz Launcelot du lake. Foz in all turneymentes and iuftes and dedes of armes / bothe foz lyfe and deth he paffed all knyghtes ⁊ at no tyme he was neuer ouercomen but yf it were by treafon oz enchauntement. Syz Launcelot encreafed fo mer uaylouffy in wozfhyp ⁊ honour / wherfoze he is the firft knyght ⁊ the frenffhe booke maketh mencyon of / after that kynge Arthur came from Rome / wher foze quene Gueneuer had hym in grete fauour aboue all other knyghtes / and certaynly he loued the quene agayne aboue all other ladyes and damoyfelles all the dayes of his lyfe / and foz her he

i ii

Malory's Morte d'Arthur *fixed our idea of King Arthur and his knights. This illustration from a 1529 edition makes no attempt to place them in the sixth century, where they really belong.*

them demonstrate how thin the line is between Arthurian fact and fiction, others are pure fraud. Was there, for instance, really a Round Table? The top of a round table hangs at Winchester Castle; and Malory associated Camelot with Winchester. But is the table top at Winchester the true Round Table? We know that the castle was built by William the Conqueror, and has no Arthurian connection.

The table at Winchester is oak, eighteen feet in diameter, and shows a painting of Arthur on a throne and holding a scepter. It is painted in an overall pattern of twenty-four alternating green and white bands or spokes. The name of a knight appears at the end of each spoke. A table eighteen feet in diameter would seat twenty-four people at most, yet Arthur's Round Table accommodated one hundred fifty knights. Such a table would have to have been 125 feet in diameter. Moreover, although the Winchester table may date from the twelfth century, its painted surface is strictly from the sixteenth century. It was commissioned by Henry VIII, probably to link his family, the Tudors, with King Arthur. Green and white were the Tudor family colors; Henry's older brother, who died before assuming the throne, was named Arthur. The Tudors, aware of their shaky claim to the English throne, found it good public relations to link their family to the legendary King Arthur.

Tintagel Castle, a crumbling ruin on the Cornish coast, is another Arthurian object of doubtful authenticity. Geoffrey of Monmouth first named it as Arthur's birthplace, but this is probably pure fancy. The existing ruin was built in the thirteenth century on the foundation of an older structure, but even the oldest known building at the site, a monastery, does not date back far enough to be truly Arthurian.

Cornwall, however, contains another object with more interesting Arthurian connections. At a crossroad one and a half miles north of the town of Fowey there stands a seven-foot stone pillar with a Latin inscription that reads: "Here lies Drustans, son of Cunomorus." Drustans is believed to be an old form of the name Tristan. Cunomorus may be a Cornish king, Marcus Quonomorius, and there is a King Mark in the Tristan story. The evidence is vague, but folk tales consistently link Tristan with Cornwall.

Between Land's End, at the western tip of Cornwall, and the Isles of Scilly there is supposed to have once been "a land of matchless grace" called Lyonesse. This British Atlantis, according to local legends, was engulfed by the sea so suddenly that only one man, riding a fast horse, escaped destruction. Malory says Lyonesse was ruled by Galahad and Tennyson places Arthur's final battle there. These are but two of its Arthurian connections. Actually, western Cornwall is filled with Arthurian associations and folk tales. But was there really a lost Lyonesse? Many scholars believe that up to Roman times southwest England extended far to the west of what is now Land's End. The engulfment of this area by the sea is geologically possible, but it would not have occurred as swiftly as the legend suggests.

In searching for Arthurian places scholars pay close attention to old place names. Where the Anglo-Saxon conquest was most complete few Celtic place names remain; where it was less complete, as in Cornwall, there are more Celtic place names in evidence. In Wales for example, where the conquest did not reach, Celtic place names are in the majority. But place names with Arthurian connections show up in northern England and Scotland. Did Arthur fight the Saxons so far from his native region? Or did the retreating Celts carry his memory with them? The place names cannot tell us as much as we would like to know.

Sometimes place names can be confusing. Camulodunum, modern Colchester, was long thought to be Camelot because of the similarity of names. But modern scholars place Camelot on a hill far to the west, in Somerset, three miles from the villages of Queen's Camel and West Camel. This hill is usually known as Cadbury Hill, but it is also called Cadbury Camp or Castle, or South Cadbury Hill, Camp, or Castle. Whatever name it is given, there is considerable evidence to support its claim as the site of Camelot.

Archaeology, history, folklore, geography, and place names all favor Cadbury Hill as the site of Camelot. The suffix "bury" is Saxon, but the prefix "Cad" has three possible Celtic connections. It could be the name of the hill's pre-Saxon owner; it could refer to the semilegendary Celtic hero Cadwy; or it could be derived from the Celtic word for "battle." Queen's Camel and West Camel are named for the Cam, the old name for a nearby stream. "Cam" is a common Celtic name for streams, and simply means "the crooked." The Celtic "Cad" and "Cam" provide links with Camelot, but other links are much stronger.

Geographically, Cadbury Hill is more likely than Colchester as the site of Camelot. It is situated at the western edge of the Saxon conquest, and near the ruins of Glastonbury Abbey, an important Arthurian site. An ancient causeway running from Cadbury Hill toward Glastonbury is known as King Arthur's Lane. There is also a King Arthur's Well at Cadbury. The area is rich in popular legends and other Arthurian associations. In fact, Cadbury Hill is right in the Heart of "Arthur country."

Cadbury is a limestone hill rising about 500 feet and topped by an Iron Age fort. It contains signs of habitation dating back about four thousand years. Archaeologists have found signs there of early Britons and Romans, as well as fragments of pottery from the eastern Mediterranean, indicating that the site was once occupied by a powerful ruler who traded with the continent. But the most interesting evidence at Cadbury Hill dates from the Dark Ages and consists of artifacts and fortifications which suggest it was used by someone of rank at roughly the time of the real Arthur. We know from the archaeological excavations that it had been used as a fort many times before, and it was used as a fort later by the Saxons. But the extensive re-fortification dating from the early sixth century suggests it was a very important fortress in southern England around the year 500. This is a strong argument for making it the site of Camelot.

In the sixteenth century Henry VIII sent his official antiquarian, John Leland, on a journey through England to prepare a kind of official guide to the realm. Leland's notes were later gathered into an *Itinerary*. "At South Cadbyri," it says, "standith Camallate, sumtyme a famose toun or castelle. The people can tell nothing thar but that they have hard say that Arture much resortid to Camalat." He goes on to record local stories; for example, that the hill was hollow and Arthur was asleep within it. On certain nights horsemen in armor would ride down from the hill to drink from a local spring. This legend remained part of the local folklore well into the nineteenth century.

William Camden, an Elizabethan antiquarian, also identified the hill as the site of Camelot. It appears as "Camelleck" on Elizabethan maps and became a popular site for visits by antiquarians, the forerunners of modern archaeologists. The finding of some graves indicated that it had been the site of a battle, and for a time it was thought to be Camlann, the scene of Arthur's last battle. By 1890, however, archaeologists were digging at Cadbury for signs of Camelot. Extensive modern digs took place in the 1950's and 1960's and in 1967 evidence was found to suggest that an important Arthur-type figure did occupy Cadbury at the right time in history.

Under a Late Saxon wall the archaeologists found the remains of an earlier rampart which dated from the late fifth or early sixth century—Arthur's time. Called the Stony Bank by the delighted archaeologists, it was clearly built to defend the home or headquarters of a major British chieftain. The archaeologists also found signs of an unfinished (or unbuilt) church, which they considered unique in Britain. It could have been either Saxon or "Arthurian."

If these dramatic finds at Cadbury predate the Saxons, if they are indeed Arthurian, then Camelot has been put on the map with some certainty. Here presumably is the fortress (and perhaps the chapel) of a great military man—the seat of power of a *dux bellorum*. Certainly no other place has been found to rival it as the site of Camelot.

Other Arthurian Places

The place names of Arthur's battles, as listed by Nennius, are no help to modern scholars. There is a forest of Celidon (the seventh battle) in Scotland, but Nennius did not indicate that any battles were fought in the north. "The City of the Legion" may be Chester or Caerleon, cities on the Welsh border that were major Roman outposts in western Britain. On the whole, identifying Nennius' place names is almost futile except for Mount Badon and Camlann.

Modern scholars put Badon at one of two sites in south-central England. One is called Badbury Rings; the other, more likely site is Liddington Hill, near Swindon Gap, about seventy miles west of London. It is a ridge, nine hundred feet high, that would have provided a most strategic encampment. There are earth ramparts on the western rise of the hill. If Arthur occupied the hill fort, and the Saxons tried to bypass him, they would have had to move through a narrow pass below the ridge. Arthur and his cavalry could have charged down and overwhelmed them. We know that the Saxons landed in southwest England and fought their way eastward along the Thames valley toward London. Liddington Hill lies along their path, and a major battle was fought somewhere along the way. The gap in the *Anglo-Saxon Chronicle* and references in Gildas' *De Excidio* indicate a great victory over the Saxons. Wherever it took place, it was a battle to remember, one that might have produced a hero of great power.

Camlann was a different sort of battle. Cornish tradition places it at Slaughter Bridge, on the Camel River near Camelford. John Leland said the local inhabitants had dug up old armor at the site, and he reported the local legend that Arthur had gone upstream from the spot mortally wounded, and had died nearby. Richard Carew's 1602 *Survey of Cornwall* describes a stone at the spot by the stream where Arthur died. There is a stone there bearing a Latin inscription, but it does not refer to Arthur. Slaughter Bridge was where the Saxons defeated the Britons in 823, and seems to have become the scene of Arthur's last battle through some kind of popular confusion. The nearby village of Camelford has also been suggested as the site of Camelot. And Camlann has been placed as far away as Scotland, near a site known as Arthur's Oven.

The name "Camlann" means "crooked enclosure," but that is not very helpful. If, as some scholars say, it is derived from Camboglanna, a fort on Hadrian's Wall, that would place the battle far from traditional Arthur country. It would also remove it from Avalon, where Arthur is supposed to have been carried after his last battle. The Isle of Avalon comes straight out of Celtic myths about an island burial place for fallen heroes. There it is usually known as the Island of Blessed Souls and is described as an earthly paradise somewhere in the western seas. "Avalon" is a Celtic name meaning "the island of apples." This Celtic romance about Avalon fits in with the notion of a "once and future king." Perhaps to overcome such an association, some opportunistic monks suggested that Arthur was really buried at Glastonbury. And with Glastonbury we come to a whole new aspect of the Arthurian story.

Glastonbury and the Holy Grail

Glastonbury Tor is a high hill dominating the surrounding countryside, which is largely marshland. Atop this hill, in very early Christian times, stood some kind of church. Glastonbury has long been a place of legends associated with Avalon, the Holy Grail, and other Arthurian elements. A mile away is the "Bridge Perilous" over the Brue River where Arthur, afer his last battle, flung his sword Excalibur into the water, and twelve miles away is Cadbury, the presumed site of Camelot.

According to legend, Joseph of Arimathea came to Britain in A.D. 63 to convert the people to Christianity. He is supposed to have carried with him the Holy Grail—the sacred chalice of the Last Supper, in which some of Christ's blood was collected at the Crucifixion. When Joseph stopped to pray at the foot of Glastonbury Tor his staff took root and budded, a sign that he had reached his journey's end. This budding staff is supposed to have grown into the Glastonbury Thorn, which flowered every Christmas. The awed local king gave Joseph the land at Glastonbury on which to settle. There he built the first Christian church in Britain, and there he buried the Holy Grail. Irish tradition has it that St. Patrick was buried at the church in 472.

There is evidence that a very early church—a wooden structure with a straw roof—was erected at Glastonbury. Archaeologists cannot give a precise date to this ancient structure. In 1184 a church and monastery crowning Glastonbury Tor burned down. It is clear from comment at the time that the site was considered to have been a holy place for a very long time. Archaeological evidence suggests it was a Celtic sanctuary that became a Christian settlement before the Saxon conquest.

The Holy Grail is surrounded by Celtic and Christian mythology, but the Church never officially recognized it. It became linked to the Arthur story when his knights took on the great quest for the holy object. (This was a later development in the story.) The fifteenth-century windows of a church near Glastonbury picture Joseph of Arimathea carrying—not the chalice known as the Holy Grail—but two cruets containing the blood and sweat of the crucified Christ. In the fifteenth century Christian theologians were busy disclaiming the Grail story.

The idea of the Grail may have developed from the mention of a sacred vessel in pagan Celtic myths. An early Welsh poem tells us that Arthur and his knights sailed to Annwn, a Celtic otherworld like Avalon, questing for a magic cauldron. The Grail first appears in its familiar form in an early eighth-century manuscript, and then in the early ninth-century *Chronicle* of Freculfe, the bishop of Lisieux. From then on the poets made much of it.

In the late twelfth century Chrétien de Troyes gave the Grail its Christian associations. In his unfinished *Conte de Graal,* he set the knights Percival, Bors, and Lancelot on the quest that was fascinating to so many other poets. Robert de Boron specified that the Holy Grail was the chalice of the Last Supper, and added Galahad, a model of chastity and purity, to the Knights of the Round Table. Percival (or Perceval or Parzifal) was almost successful in the quest, but Galahad became the truly successful knight.

In the Arthur story the Holy Grail has definitely become the chalice of the Last Supper, containing drops of Christ's blood. It had been brought to the "Vales of Avalon" by Joseph of Arimathea or his companions, but, by Arthur's time, has been lost somewhere in Britain. It is kept in a mysterious castle surrounded by a wasteland, held by the wounded and paralyzed Fisher King. If a questing knight finds the castle and asks the right question the king will be healed and the wasteland revived. Clearly, in about four centuries, the Grail had produced its own mythology.

Though the Church disclaimed the Grail stories, the monks of Glastonbury latched onto the theme, because it served their interest. Freculfe's *Chronicle* had said that Joseph of Arimathea was given an island, Ynis Avalon, as a sanctuary. The area around Glastonbury Tor had long been a marshy region that was often completely inundated. In early accounts it was called Ynis Witrin, Isle of Glass, because the watery marsh looked like glass and the church on the Tor rose above it like an island. Soon the area was being called the Isle of Avalon, and the Glastonbury monks may have prompted, as well as approved of, the change in name. It was called an island, presumably, because of the marsh, and Avalon because it was covered with apple trees.

The monks of Glastonbury were capable of making the most of any legend that came their way. In 1189 King Henry II was busy helping the monks rebuild at Glastonbury after the disastrous fire of 1184. A few years later, when Henry was safely dead, it was said that he had been at Glastonbury because he had learned from a Welsh bard that Arthur was buried there. This story was reported by Giraldus Cambrensis (Gerald of Wales) at about the time the monks of Glastonbury ran out of money for their rebuilding project. Then they made a very convenient discovery. While excavating at the site they uncovered the bodies of Arthur and Guinevere.

Their grave was marked by a lead cross inscribed: "Here lies buried the renowned King Arthur, with Guinevere his second wife, in the Isle of Avalon." The remains were examined by Edward I in a special Easter ceremony in 1278; a Glastonbury monk was on hand to describe the scene. The bodies were lost by Tudor times, though Tudor antiquarians described the famous grave. The epitaph varies in these accounts, and one version even includes the Once and Future King inscription. (This is odd, because it contradicts the need of the Plantagenet kings to have Arthur safely dead and buried; but it could have served Tudor interests.)

How reliable is the connection between Glastonbury and Avalon? Archaeological evidence puts a Christian settlement at the site before the Saxons and after the Celts. This suggests that a leader like Arthur could have been buried at a long-hallowed place like Glastonbury—but it proves nothing. The inscribed cross, which Giraldus says he held in his own hands, was preserved at Glastonbury into Elizabethan times. William Camden reprinted its inscription in 1607 as: "Here lies Arthur, the famous king, in the island of Avalon." This version differs from Giraldus', particularly in not mentioning Guinevere. Did one of them misquote the inscription? Or did Camden see something other than the cross held by Giraldus? A tomb was rediscovered during excavations in 1931, presumably the one described by Giraldus, but by then the cross had disappeared.

The connection between Glastonbury and Avalon can be traced pretty clearly to Giraldus. Earlier in the twelfth century Geoffrey of Monmouth mentioned Avalon without relating it to Glastonbury. Moreover, he made no mention of Joseph of Arimathea or the Grail. Then too, in a *Life of St. Gildas,* written about 1150, Guinevere is said to have been abducted and held at Glastonbury. Arthur comes to rescue her and afterward he remains there to pray. In this Arthurian story Glastonbury appears as Ynis Witrin, the Isle of Glass. So, less than fifty years before Giraldus' report, the Avalon connection has not been made.

The principal early authority on Glastonbury is William of Malmesbury, who visited there in 1125. His book, *On the Antiquity of the Church of Glastonbury,* exists in a copy dating from 1140 and a re-edited version of about a century later. A comparison between the two texts shows how a hundred or so years can alter a popular legend. Arthur is not mentioned in connection with Glastonbury in the early version, but the connection is made in the *later* version, in a part of the text scholars feel is not really by William. The later version, of course, comes after Giraldus.

William would not have supported the Avalon theory about Glastonbury. "The tomb of Arthur is nowhere beheld," he wrote, "whence the ancient ditties fable that he is yet to come." Nor did he believe the Joseph of Arimathea story, preferring another account that dated the church from A.D. 166. Joseph's journey to Britain cannot be proved or disproved. He is described in the Gospels as a rich merchant. Certainly it was possible for such a person to travel from Palestine to Britain in the first century A.D. But most of the Joseph of Arimathea story is apocryphal and legendary, and not actually in the Bible. The monks of Glastonbury said he arrived there with two glass containers holding the blood and sweat of Christ. They did not mention the Grail, but probably because of the Church's official attitude toward that object. The Grail, also, is a late addition to the story.

William of Malmesbury's account of the church seems reasonable to most scholars. Glastonbury was one of the most holy shrines in Britain in his day; certainly it was ancient, and saints probably had visited it. That it was anything more is unlikely. William believed in Arthur's existence, and would have mentioned the Avalon connection if he had known of it. He refers to Glastonbury as Ynis Witrin, not Ynis Avalon. The Avalon connection is Giraldus' contribution, and it appears conveniently after the fire that set the Glastonbury monks on their money-raising venture. But the monks cannot be blamed for capitalizing on a good story! The kings of England were just as willing to make it serve their own purposes.

Modern scholarship may have debunked Glastonbury's claim to be Avalon, but archaeologists are examining fortifications at Cadbury with great enthusiasm. While scholars discuss cavalry charges at Liddington Hill and scientists pursue the real Arthur, writers continue to create popular romances on Arthurian themes. Most of us, in one way or another, are willing to believe in Camelot.

EIGHT

Prester John

I N the year 1165 a most unusual letter was delivered to the
Christian world's three most powerful rulers—the By-
zantine Emperor Manuel, the Holy Roman Emperor Freder-
ick Barbarossa, and Pope Alexander III. It is not known who
sent or delivered the three letters, though they probably
came from somewhere in the East. We do know that the
same text was delivered to each ruler and that it was written in Latin. Even though everything else about the letter
remains a mystery, it set off a three-hundred-year search for
a completely mythical kingdom.

The text comes down to us from copies of the By-
zantine emperor's letter. It opens with a formal greeting
from "Presbyter Johannes" to "his friend Emanuel, Prince
of Constantinople." The tone of the letter is boastful: "I,
Prester John, the Lord of Lords, surpass all the rulers of the
earth in wealth, virtue and power. Seventy-two kings pay
tribute to us." Prester John states that his dominions extend
to India and that only a few of his seventy-two provinces

are Christian. Then the letter goes on the describe Prester John's kingdom.

It is a land filled with elephants, camels, panthers, lions, tigers, gryphons, wild horses, and other animals. It also contains wild people, horned people, one-eyed people, centaurs, fauns, satyrs, pygmies, giants, cyclopes, the phoenix, and all sorts of other creatures. We recognize this catalogue of wonders as being the traditional European view of Eastern fauna introduced by Pliny. If anyone noticed the similarity at the time it would not have been remarked upon. For more than a thousand years nobody doubted the accuracy of Pliny's account.

Next the letter takes up Prester John's magnificent court. He is waited on by kings, primates, archbishops, bishops, and abbots. Surrounded by such titled people, he prefers to be called simply Prester (Priest) "out of humility." Every day this humble priest's table, made of emeralds and standing on pillars of amethyst, is set for thirty thousand people. He is served by seven kings, sixty-two dukes and two hundred and sixty-five counts. His palace is built of gems held together by gold. The roof is made of sapphires and topazes; the gate, made of crystal bound with gold, opens and closes by itself when he enters the palace.

Only the Pope responded to the letter. About twelve years later, he sent a guarded and diplomatic reply from Venice. He did not mention "the holy priest" by name. In fact, about all he said was that he would send Magister Philippus to Prester John's kingdom to teach Catholic doctrine. And he would do this only if messengers returned with a reply. The Philip referred to was the Pope's physician, who had contacts with "many persons in the East." He may or may not have delivered the Pope's message, assuming that he knew where to deliver it. In any event, after this brief mention, he seems to have dropped out of the story.

Why did the Pope answer Prester John's letter, even after a twelve-year delay? The explanation is simply that Christian Europe was quite willing to believe in the existence of Prester John. There were numerous reasons for this, as we shall see. Not the least of these reasons was that Prester John's name was already known in Europe at the time of the letter.

Some years earlier a mysterious Eastern visitor had arrived in Rome. He was known as "John Patriarch of the Indians" or, in some accounts, as simply "an archbishop of India." He came to Rome in 1122, supposedly after a year's journey, asking to see Pope Calixtus II. He stayed for a year, telling wonderful stories about India. Most particularly, he told of a magnificent tomb, the Shrine of St. Thomas. This saint, one of the original Apostles, was supposed to have traveled to India after the Crucifixion to preach the gospel. Miracles were said to occur daily at his magnificent tomb. After a year, Patriarch John, who was presumably an imposter as well as a good storyteller, simply disappeared.

In 1145 another visitor to Rome provided a stronger link with the Prester John of the 1165 letter. He was Bishop Hugh of Jabala, a Syrian town near Antioch. His region had been overrun by the Moslems and he came to Rome to appeal for help from Pope Eugenius III. There he met Bishop Otto of Freising, a noted historian of the time. Bishop Otto recorded Hugh's story of "a certain John, a king and priest who dwells beyond Persia and Armenia." This account describes John as a descendant of the Magi, who was living in great wealth and glory. He was a Christian who had defeated the Persians in battle and who hoped "to fight for the Church at Jerusalem." Unfortunately, so far he had been unable to get his army across the Tigris River.

It is believed that Hugh's story refers to a battle fought near Samarkand, in which the Moslems of central Asia were defeated by the ruler of a country known as Black Cathay. This ruler was probably a Buddhist whose forces may have included Nestorian Christians. (The Nestorians were followers of Nestorius, who died in 451. He was a Syrian priest, for many years Patriarch of Constantinople, who was banished for heresy.) If Pope Alexander connected Prester John with the Nestorians it may explain why he wanted to instruct the priest in Catholic doctrine.

The idea of a Moslem defeat by a Christian leader in Asia is what really lies at the heart of the Prester John legend. But the Christian leader was no Charlemagne, not even a Western-style Crusader. He was Yeliutashi, the chieftain of the Kerait people, also known as the Karakhitai or "Black Chinese." The great battle he won was fought on September 8 and 9, 1141, at Katvan, near Samarkand. Though he is thought to have been a Buddhist, Yeliutashi may have been a Nestorian, like many of his subjects. The possibility of his being a Christian and the dates of his reign make it likely that he was the figure in Hugh of Jabala's story.

In 1145, the year Hugh called on Pope Eugenius, the Pope was issuing the call for the second Crusade. Thus a Christian victory over Moslems in a great battle in Asia was of considerable interest. The collapse of the Crusade and the increased threat from Moslem armies between 1145 and 1165 made a victorious priest-king all the more attractive to Christian Europe. The connection between the imposter Patriarch John, Hugh's priest-king named John and the Prester John of the 1165 letter may seem very slim to us now. But in the twelfth century the willingness to connect them with each other and with the victorious Yeliutashi would not be so unlikely.

In the thirteenth century travelers began bringing back stories of Prester John and his kingdom. One of these was the Franciscan monk, Friar Giovanni de Piano Carpini, who traveled in the East between 1245 and 1247. He reported that Genghis Khan had sent his son, Ogotay, to fight the "Black Indians," or "Saracens also called Ethiopians." They beat back Ogotay's men, said Carpini, with new weapons of the Christian king called Prester John. The principal new weapon, however, sounds very much like the ancient "Greek fire," burning sulfur and pitch.

The French monk, Friar William of Rubrouck, whom we have also mentioned before, traveled to the East as an envoy of his king from 1253 to 1255. He later wrote that, in a plain in the highlands of central Asia, "there lived a Nestorian shepherd, being a mighty governor over the people called Naimans." After the death of "Con Khan" this shepherd made himself ruler of the kingdom. The people called him "King John" and exaggerated his greatness. Exaggeration, says William, was typical of the Nestorians of those parts. He also informs us that John's brother, "Unc," was ruler in "Caracorum" and was defeated by Genghis Khan.

Marco Polo, who traveled through the East from 1271 to 1295, says Prester John and Unc Khan were the same person. Marco Polo's *Travels* contains several mentions of Prester John. There were also references to the land of Prester John in the early fourteenth century. One was in the travel report of Friar Odoric of Pordenone, the Franciscan monk who undertook a six-year journey through China in 1318. But, until Sir John Mandeville, the principal writer on Prester John remained Marco Polo.

Marco Polo's Stories of Prester John

From Marco Polo we learn of Prester John's association with the Tartars, but not much else. There are in the *Travels* some brief references to Prester John, the description of a province ruled by one of his descendants, and two entertaining and instructive stories about events in the time of John's reign. However, the central character could be any oriental king, or even Charlemagne or Arthur.

According to Marco Polo, the Tartars were bound in tribute to Prester John, "of whose great empire all the world speaks." When he saw how they had grown in numbers and power, Prester John tried to divide the Tartars among several countries. As soon as they discovered his intention "they departed in a body and went into a desert place toward the north." There they held out as rebels, and there Genghis Khan united them. When Genghis finally ruled many people over a large area "he made up his mind to conquer a great part of the world."

In the year 1200, says Marco Polo, Genghis Khan sent emissaries to Prester John asking to marry his daughter. Prester John refused the request, saying that Genghis was a traitor. Genghis Khan was enraged by this insult and decided to demonstrate who was the more powerful lord. He assembled a vast army, and "with all his followers, entered a wide and pleasant plain called Tenduk, which belonged to Prester John, and there encamped. And I assure you that they were such a multitude that their number was beyond count." There followed what Marco Polo calls "the greatest battle that was ever seen." Not only did Genghis Khan win, but Prester John was killed and all his lands were subdued by Genghis.

Tenduk (or Tenduc) is thought to be Mongolia, one of the provinces described by Marco Polo. It contains many towns and villages, and its chief city is also called Tenduk. Here Prester John had his principal residence "when he was lord of the Tartars." The province, which produces lapis lazuli in abundance, is also involved in agriculture, commerce, and industry. Marco Polo briefly describes its natives, handsome, intelligent people who appeal to him, probably because they are businessmen. The inhabitants of the province, he says, are subjects of the Great Khan and include descendants of Prester John. The local ruler is a Christian priest named George, who carries the title "Prester John." He is the sixth ruler in descent from the original priest-king. A vassal of the Great Khan, he rules less land than the first Prester John.

"This is the place," says Marco Polo, "which we call in our language Gog and Magog; the natives call it Ung and Mungul." In Ung, he continues, live the Gog, in Mungul the Tartars. The land of Gog and Magog appears on medieval maps, but the original Gog and Magog appear in the Bible in quite different forms. In *Revelation* they are symbolic of all the future enemies of the Kingdon of God. In *Ezekiel* Gog is the ruler of Magog; a tyrant of a northern country, probably Armenia; by the seventh century Gog had become identified with the Antichrist. According to many medieval legends this Man of Sin was supposed to precede the second coming of Christ. Marco Polo's Prester John, ruler of Gog and Magog, is a curious Christian hero and a far cry from Hugh of Jabala's priest-king.

The second story, about the Golden King, is probably the work of Marco Polo's literary collaborator. The Golden King is subject to Prester John but has made war on him; Prester John cannot subdue him, which makes him very angry. Seven henchmen of Prester John say they will bring him the Golden King as a prisoner. This is a conventional beginning to a medieval story and what follows is equally unoriginal.

The seven henchmen and a party of servants travel to the court of the Golden King, saying they have come from a far country to enter his service. Two years after joining his court they have won his high regard. One day the Golden

King goes out hunting with a small party that includes the seven men he has come to trust. After separating themselves from the rest of the group, the seven henchmen seize the king. They tell him they will either kill him or bring him "to our lord and master, Prester John."

The Golden King is brought to Prester John who orders him sent out as a cowherd. Under close watch, he is kept at this lowly task for two years and is then summoned again to Prester John, who dresses him in rich robes and treats him with honor. Now, says Prester John, the Golden King can see he is not the man to make war against him. The humbled king agrees "there is no man who can stand against you." Because he has admitted this, says Prester John, the Golden King will be sent back to his country with honor. "And the king returned to his own kingdom and from that time onward remained a faithful friend and vassal to his overlord."

Mandeville's Prester John

The legend of Prester John was kept alive by Sir John Mandeville, who said he had visited the priest-king's fabulous land. We know, of course, that Mandeville's travels were fictitious, but to his contemporaries they were as real as Marco Polo's. Mandeville's picture of the kingdom of Prester John fitted the popular image set by the letter of 1165, and it added details that were convincing to gullible audiences. Considering the popularity of Mandeville's *Travels*, it is likely that his picture was the accepted fourteenth-century view of Prester John's mysterious kingdom.

In Mandeville's version, Prester John's vast empire seems to be the same country as India. It is rich, says the knight, but not as rich as Cathay, nor is it as easy to reach or to trade with. Discussing trade routes allows him to throw in a frightening description of magnetic rocks that lure any ship made with iron nails. He tells how to reach Prester John's kingdom overland as well, tracing a route past Persia and cities called Hermes and Soboth (or Colach) and through a land filled with parrots.

Mandeville says "Prester John and the Great Khan of Tartary are evermore allied together through marriage, for either of them weds other daughter or other sister." The emperor is a Christian, "and the most part of his land also." In his land are a great many different precious stones, some so large that cups and plates are made from them. This description echoes the letter of 1165, and Mandeville also repeats the original claim that seventy-two kings serve under the rule of Prester John. Then he tells of the marvels in Prester John's land. The first of these is "a great sea all of gravel and sand, and no drop of water therein." It ebbs and flows, is absolutely impassable, and contains delicious fish of strange shapes, even though "there be no water in that sea." He confirms this by saying he ate these fish, so surely it is true.

Three days' journey from this sea are mountains "out of the which comes a great river that comes from Paradise, and it is full of precious stones and no drop of water." Beyond lies a sandy plain with trees that spring up at dawn, bear fruit at midday, and dwindle and disappear at sunset. Nobody can eat or even touch the fruit; "for it seems as it were a phantom and a deceivable thing to the sight." This "marvellous thing" is clearly a fanciful description based on the phenomenon of mirages. The wilderness also contains "many wild men with horns upon their heads," and wild animals, including talking birds, the *psitakes* or parrots mentioned earlier.

After a description of Prester John riding into battle

carrying enormous gold crosses, Mandeville's invention seems to falter. He turns to John's palace in the city of Susa—"so rich, so delectable, so noble . . ." But his description only elaborates upon the one in the 1165 letter. He tells of another palace in the city of Nise, where the air is not as wholesome as in Susa. The description of Prester John's court that follows is once again drawn from the 1165 letter. And Mandeville's comment that the priest-king is "full richly served and worshipfully" is an uncharacteristic understatement.

Mandeville concludes by stating that Prester John's land "lasts on breadth four months journey and on length it is without measure." Then he repeats that everything he has said is true: "Trow all this, for sickerly I saw it with mine eyes and mickle more than I have told you. For my fellows and I were dwelling with him in his court a long time and saw all this that I have told you and mickle more than I have leisure for to tell." Believe this, he says, because I tell you I saw it all, and much more. Oddly enough, his audience did believe it, and for no other reason than that he said it was so.

A Movable Kingdom

Belief in Prester John's kingdom was hard to discourage. Prince Henry the Navigator sent his Portuguese captains in search of it. Most Europeans were convinced that it existed somewhere in the East; at one point Vasco da Gama thought he had found it. On landing at Mozambique he wrote: "We were told that Prester John resided not far from this place; that he held many cities along the coast and the inhabitants of these cities were great merchants and owned big ships." Mozambique, on the southeastern coast of Africa facing Madagascar, was not Prester John's kingdom. But, as mentioned earlier, it may have been Punt.

The opening up of India and the rest of Asia did not finish off Prester John's mythical kingdom. The Portuguese explorers simply moved it to East Africa. As a matter of fact, in the reign of John II (1481–1495) Portugal actually sent missions to Prester John in East Africa. Pedro de Covilhão, better known by his Latin name, Petrus Covillanius, seems to have been responsible for this. When Covillanius reached Abyssinia (modern Ethiopia) he found it a mysterious mountainous country that stretched beyond sight. He also found it populated by dark-skinned Christians whose ruler traced his line back to the Biblical King David. Covillanius easily convinced himself that he had found the land of Prester John. He also convinced a great many other people. Years later, when an envoy from the Emperor of Abyssinia arrived at the court of the Portuguese King, he was greeted as an emissary from Prester John. The idea that Abyssinia was the realm of Prester John remained in some people's minds for at least three centuries.

A fourteenth-century Dominican friar, Jordanus de Severac, had apparently been the first person to move Prester John to East Africa, so the Portuguese misconception about

Part of Africa, from a 1598 map. By this time Prester John's constantly moving kingdom had finally settled in Abyssinia (Ethiopia).

Ethiopia (or Abyssinia) was not without some basis. Then, too, there was the Ptolemaic notion that Ethiopia and India were connected. In much of the popular geography of medieval times the Nile separated Africa from Asia. It was not unusual to find Ethiopia and India confused with each other in some accounts.

The idea for moving Prester John to Africa may have been based on an old story. In the ninth century a North African Jewish scholar told of a kingdom of the "Sons of Moses." It was made up of four of the Ten Lost Tribes of Israel, and was situated somewhere beyond "the rivers of Ethiopia." Some scholars offer another explanation of the connection to Ethiopia. They say the Ethiopian title *zan* was confused with the name "John," and everything grew out of this simple mistake.

The significant point, however, is that India was opened up and Prester John's kingdom had to be moved elsewhere. A 1507 map places his realm in "Thebet" (Tibet). A legend on the map states: "This is the land of the good King and lord, known as Prester John, lord of all Eastern and Southern India, lord of all the kings of India, in whose mountains are found all kinds of precious stones."

Some Possible Sources

Let us return to the letter of 1165. Nothing that followed it

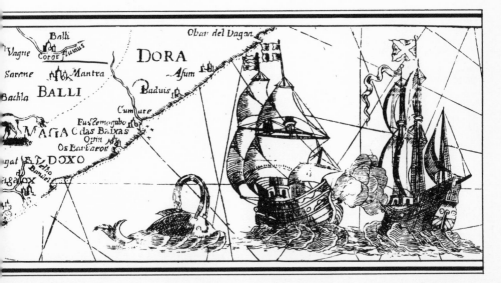

for centuries added to the original material, except to fill in fanciful details. Who wrote the letter and why? Most of the information in the letter has been traced by scholars to books that were current in Europe at the time. But some of the information was not in circulation in twelfth-century Europe. This interesting fact suggests to some modern scholars a possible author. They think he must have been some European who had been to the East, possibly on the Second Crusade (1147–1149), which had failed. A disillusioned participant of that Crusade seems the most likely author.

But why was the letter written? It may have been what we call a Utopian work—offering a theory that is ideal and visionary. Prester John's ideal state was obviously superior to twelfth-century Europe. His Utopian kingdom was ruled by a simple mortal priest more powerful and more divine than the European rulers who declared themselves divine. All the wealth of this magnificent kingdom belonged to everyone. Unlike Europe, in Prester John's realm there was perpetual peace, tranquility, law, and freedom. In short, Prester John's land was everything Europe was not.

Another theory is that the letter was written to give hope to Europeans of finding a Christian ally in the East, which would help in mounting a new Crusade. A third theory, not directly related to the letter, says that Prester John is part of the Nestorian legend. The followers of Nestorius were evangelists who founded Christian communities from Syria all the way to China, living among the Mongols and even Moslems. They were, as we know, considered heretical Christians. The Nestorians traced themselves to St. Thomas, who is credited with conversions, miracles, and eventual martyrdom in India. He appears in the apocryphal *Acts of St. Thomas*, written in the third or fourth century.

The Nestorians are supposed to have kept alive a whole body of stories about St. Thomas, and according to these stories Thomas had a son named Vizan. A modern scholar, Vsevolod Slessarev, says that over the years the name was rewritten as "John." Vizan, legend has it, assumed the role of leader of the Indian Christians. In the twelfth century the nearest major Christian community in Asia was at Samarkand. And so the locale of the Vizan or "John" stories was moved by Europeans with a faint knowledge of Nestorian legends.

How credible is this Nestorian link? The Moslems destroyed the Nestorian library at Edessa, and the bulk of their literature has been lost. In the fourteenth century Tamerlane and the Tartars practically destroyed the whole faith, and whatever remained of Nestorian writing was scattered and lost in Oriental archives. There is always the possibility that some day a connecting link between Prester John and the Nestorians will be uncovered in some long lost manuscript. Until then it is just as reasonable to say Prester John was created for propaganda purposes.

NINE

El Dorado

AFTER Columbus it was only a matter of time before a New World Neverland would make its appearance. There were two principal reasons for this. One was that the world was expanding rapidly, and distance was taking on new meaning. Far places had to be so much farther away. The sea route from Spain to Mexico was almost double the mileage of the land route from Constantinople to India. The age of discovery introduced the Europeans to an unexpectedly large and watery world.

The other reason for locating Neverland in the New World was gold. In 1519 Hernando Cortez conquered Mexico, and in the 1530's Francisco Pizarro conquered Peru. But Mexico and Peru were not Neverlands, and their treasures of gold were definitely real. However, the gold of the Americas was about to create a whole new mythological geography. After Mexico and Peru, what could be more reasonable than to discover a third realm of gold?

The great barrier to exploration was the sea, approximately three-fourths of the earth's surface. Once the sea was crossed and new continents were discovered, exploration would proceed at a rapid pace. Renaissance Europe was driven by its desperate need for gold and spices. Gold was always convenient to have, but the spices were of greater importance to Europe than we might realize. They were needed to make food edible, not just tasty. As a result, Europe in the fifteenth century burst out of its closed and narrow world. And what the explorers of Renaissance Europe opened up was truly a New World—continents larger than the one from which they came. In such a New World there was room for more than one Neverland.

In 1528 Pánfilo de Narváez and four hundred settlers landed near Tampa in the hope of finding the gold regions rumored to be there. Having lost their ships almost immediately, they marched northward along Florida's west coast. Not only did they not find any gold, but everything seems to have gone wrong for them. When about a third of the party was dead, largely from starvation, they decided to build new ships and sail for Mexico. They built five ships and lost four of them off the mouth of the Mississippi River. The survivors, only eighty of the original four hundred, reached land near what is now Galveston, Texas. By spring only fifteen of them were alive.

The leader of the survivors was Álvar Núñez Cabeza de Vaca. He and his men wandered with various tribes of poor Indians for six years. Cabeza de Vaca proved to be most adaptable and resourceful while living with these primitive nomads. Finally, in 1536, he and three other survivors returned to Mexico with a party of Spanish raiders. For all his adventures and hardships, he had nothing to show—but he did have something to tell. It was a report of seven golden cities, later known as the Seven Cities of Cibola, just north of the area in which he had been wandering.

When Cabeza de Vaca returned to Spain he told his friend Hernando de Soto about the seven cities. He also spoke of the great wealth of the Mississippi valley. In 1539 de Soto led a party of six hundred men into this supposed realm of gold. In four years the expedition covered 350,000 square miles of the southeastern and southwestern United States. De Soto died on the expedition and was buried in the Mississippi. About half his men survived, but they found no golden cities.

The Seven Cities of Cibola "moved" farther West. Other Spanish adventurers came up from Mexico, into what is now our Southwest, in search of them. One expedition into Arizona was guided by a Moorish slave, Estevan, who had survived with Cabeza de Vaca. As early as 1540 their route was followed by Francisco Vásquez de Coronado. He wintered near what is now Santa Fe, and then sent out parties in all directions looking for the Seven Cities of Cibola. (One of these groups discovered the Grand Canyon.) Coronado crossed what are now Texas and Oklahoma, reaching as far as eastern Kansas, in search of Quivara—another supposedly wealthy region that proved remarkably elusive. It was always some place beyond where it was supposed to be once Coronado got there.

Coronado's expedition never found anything more exciting than pueblos, except for the Grand Canyon—poor pueblos instead of golden cities, but most scholars think these unusual dwellings prompted the Cibola legend. Meanwhile, another legend was in the making that would prove to be more fascinating—El Dorado.

The Search for El Dorado

El Dorado ranks with Prester John and Atlantis as one of Western man's more enduring myths. It began as the myth of a gilded man, and in time the name shifted from the man to the place where he lived. Like many other myths, it had a counterpart. In this case it was the Rio Doro, the River of Gold, which was supposed to exist somewhere in Africa. Its mouth was said to be near Cape Bojador, and the river reportedly flowed through the region called Bilad Ghana. Cape Bojador, on the northwest coast of Africa, lies off the Canary Islands. Bilad Ghana, roughly Guinea, is the region to the south. According to the Arab geographer Idrisi, it was a land of fabulous wealth. The basis for the story of this mythical river was probably some vague and confused account of the Niger or Senegal River, brought back by Arab caravans in North Africa.

A River of Gold sounds as unreal as a Fountain of Youth. But there were two good reasons for believing in a Golden Man in the sixteenth century. For one thing, the gold of the Americas was not only real but abundant. For another, the gilded man was the central figure of a perfectly plausible native ritual. And yet he was a glorious myth, an American Prester John, according to the scholar Boies Penrose. Professor Penrose has noted the similarities between the El Dorado and Prester John legends. Most striking is the way each figure is relocated as the explorers pursue him. In both legends, says Penrose, "fact was elaborated into fiction in the most unblushing fashion."

As it moved from a lake near Bogotá to the Orinoco jungles, the El Dorado story grew. El Dorado himself changed from a native chieftain to a mighty ruler like Prester John. His town on Lake Guatavitá grew into a fabulous city with streets paved with gold. He became, in Professor Penrose's words, "that elusive will-o'-the-wisp, the Gilded Man, who lived in the golden city of Manoa on the shores of the fabled lake of Parima." And it all happened in a remarkably short time.

A fanciful depiction of the entrance to the palace of El Dorado. The Moorish and African trappings are entirely wrong; but then, El Dorado was entirely imaginary.

It was in Quito that the Spanish first heard the story. They were told of a tribe far to the north that practiced an unusual ritual. When a new chief was installed, the tribe conducted an elaborate ceremony at nearby Lake Guatavitá. Painted men covered with feathers, jaguar skins, gold, and emeralds, accompanied by their priests, led the new chief to the sacred lake. The chief, who was naked, was carried in a cart richly adorned with gold. But during the ceremony his body was covered with sticky resins and pure gold dust was blown onto him. He became *el hombre dorado,* "the Gilded Man." Then he and his followers took a balsa raft to the middle of the lake, where he dove into the water and washed off his gold covering while his companions tossed gold and jewels into the lake. Afterward there was much dancing and feasting in the streets of Guatavitá.

There were three paths that the explorers took in search of El Dorado. One went northeast from Quito, in Ecuador; another went south from Santa Marta, on what is now the northern coast of Colombia; and the third moved westward from Venezuela and the mouth of the Orinoco River. One of the first seekers after El Dorado, Diego de Ordaz, originally tried to find him by way of the Amazon. After suffering a shipwreck, this veteran of Cortez's army moved to the Orinoco.

Ordaz began his search in 1531. Once he reached the mouth of the Orinoco he proceeded upriver for a considerable distance. Ignoring native advice to follow a navigable tributary, the Meta River, he eventually found his way blocked. Ordaz found no sign of El Dorado, though he covered a thousand miles of the Orinoco basin. This failure did not stop his lieutenant, Alonso de Herrera, from taking up the search. Herrera journeyed up the Orinoco in 1533, and switched to the Meta as the natives advised. Unfortunately, he was killed by an Indian's poisoned arrow and the expedition returned empty-handed in 1535.

Meanwhile, the Germans had entered into the search for El Dorado. The unlikely entrance of these northern Europeans came about through the activities of a family of merchant bankers, the Welsers. Charles V, who ruled Germany as well as Spain, was deeply in debt to the Welsers, so he paid them off with patents, or land grants, to Venezuela. Given a piece of the New World to exploit for their own gain, the Welsers sent an agent to Venezuela in 1531.

Ambrose Ehinger, or Alfinger, as the Spanish records call him, led an expedition from Coro westward past Lake Maracaibo, over the mountains into Colombia, to the Magdalena River. His cruelty so enraged the natives that they attacked his party all the way back along his return route. Ehinger was killed, and only a few survivors returned to Coro in 1533. Two years later another German adventurer, George von Speier—Hohemut in the Spanish records—set out from Coro. By this time the El Dorado story was being widely circulated. Von Speier went south from Coro, kept east of the Andes, and finally reached a point practically on the equator. At the village of La Fragua he discovered a temple of the sun, which convinced him he was close to El Dorado. But, after cutting their way through about fifteen hundred miles of jungle, von Speier and his men returned to Coro without having found the elusive Gilded Man.

Nicholas Federmann, who was supposed to reinforce von Speier, involved himself instead in one of the most fascinating coincidences of exploration. Federmann should have followed von Speier south, but he took off across the Andes in the direction of Bogotá. At the same time a Spaniard named Belalcazar was leading an expedition up from Quito. Another Spanish expedition, headed by Gonzalo Jiménez de Quesada, set off down the route from Santa Marta. All three parties, from Venezuela, Quito, and Santa Marta, were in search of El Dorado. And all three were headed for exactly the same place.

Quesada was a young lawyer from Spain who joined an expedition that Alonso de Lugo led inland from Santa Marta in 1535. A year later he headed his own large expedition inland in search of the wealthy places that were supposed to be there. Actually, he was going into a land of steaming tropical jungles broken only by rugged hills. This terrible region was populated by hostile natives and hordes of insects. Tropical diseases, borne by insects, would prove a much worse threat than Indian poisoned arrows.

He set out in April, 1536, with nine hundred men. For some reason, he divided the party into two groups. One was to travel on the Magdalena River and the other overland, keeping to the left of the river. The river group met with continual disasters, and few of them ever returned to Santa Marta. The overland group, under Quesada's leadership, met with its own share of disasters. For one thing, Quesada had chosen to fight his way through forests and swamps during the rainy season. In eight months he managed to cover about three hundred miles. He reached Vélez, less than five hundred miles from Santa Marta, in just under a year. Only a hundred and sixty-six men remained in his party.

They were now in the uplands. It remained part of the legend that El Dorado would be found on a high plateau. Quesada and his men fought the local natives and conquered the area. In August, 1537, he founded the city of Bogotá, which he named Santa Fé. His conquests greatly extended the colony known as New Granada. As Bogotá, his city would become the nucleus of the expanded colony. Quesada was certain he had discovered a wealthy region, and he established control promptly. His promptness was well taken. When Belalcazar arrived from Quito and Federmann from Venezuela, Quesada was firmly in control.

The three explorers met at Bogotá in February, 1539. They tried to settle their disputed claims by appealing to Charles V. Meanwhile, Quesada strengthened his hold upon the region. At the same time he did not forget El Dorado. His brother led a combined group of adventurers to Lake Guatavitá, but there they found no sign of the fabled ceremony. They had reached the right place and there was no Gilded Man. It was time for El Dorado to move to another unexplored region.

El Dorado Moves East

After Quesada the search moved eastward, to where the Meta River meets the Orinoco. At the same time the El

Dorado legend was magnified. The initiation ceremony of the Gilded Man became a daily occurrence. Soon all his nobles and priests were gilded as well. Gradually El Dorado grew into the name of a region, not just a man, becoming a country where gold lay all around just waiting to be picked up.

The search for El Dorado produced some unexpected results. In 1536 Gonzalo de Pineda led an expedition out of Quito, across the mountains, to what became known as the Land of Cinnamon. In 1539 he was followed by Gonzalo Pizarro, half brother of the man who had conquered the Incas. Pizarro left Quito with two hundred soldiers, four thousand Indians and a large herd of animals. Eventually this major expedition reached the headwaters of the Curaray River in northern Ecuador, which flows into others that finally become the mighty Amazon. But Pizarro had no idea of this. His party was in such desperate condition that survival was their only real concern.

They built a small ship and divided their remaining forces. Pizarro took charge of the land party and put his lieutenant, Francisco de Orellana, in charge of fifty-three men aboard the ship. Orellana was supposed to follow along behind Pizarro and his men, but the river was swift and the ship soon outdistanced Pizarro. Orellana waited for a time for Pizarro to catch up to him, though he is often accused of having deserted his leader. In the end Pizarro struggled back to Quito, while Orellana built a second ship and stuck to the river.

On August 26, 1541, eight months after leaving Pizarro, Orellana's two vessels reached the mouth of the river and sailed out into the Atlantic. Using blankets as sails, they voyaged along the coast. Finally, "without either pilot, compass, or anything useful for navigation," as Orellana put it, they reached the island of Cubagua. The journey was actually rather uneventful. But Orellana's Dominican friar,

Carvajal, wrote a colorful account of it and included the story of a fight with a party of female Indians. The story was ridiculed, but Carvajal's reference to classical female warriors had a lasting effect. The river has been known ever since as the Amazon.

In 1541 Philip von Hutten also headed south from Coro. Von Hutten, the last of the German adventurers in the New World, attacked a town that was supposed to be filled with golden idols. It was filled instead with hostile natives. The survivors, including a badly wounded von Hutten, returned to Venezuela, marking the end of Germany's explorations in America. That same year Herman Pérez de Quesada led an expedition in search of El Dorado. This Quesada was the younger brother of Bogotá's founder. Starting from Tunja, near Bogotá, he crossed the Andes and traveled southeast. He was back in a year, having lost half his men.

The journeys in search of El Dorado were too numerous for us to consider all of them. They occupied years, wasted countless lives, were fruitless (except to expand geographical knowledge), and served only to move the location of El Dorado to the backlands of Guiana. The elusive Gilded Man was coming to rest in one of the most inaccessible regions on earth. Fittingly, the search was taken up by an adventurer who was something of a Don Quixote.

Antonio de Berrio led the the first of his three expeditions in search of El Dorado in 1584. A brave and stubborn explorer, he was a soldier in his sixties who had married the niece of Jiménez de Quesada. His first expedition took him from Tunja to the Orinoco. He returned because the area was too fever-ridden to continue the search. His second expedition took him from Colombia to the mountains east of the Orinoco. This time he returned because a mutiny put an end to the expedition.

By 1590 El Dorado had been officially proclaimed a

Spanish colony and Berrio was named its governor. All he had to do was find it. He set out from Tunja in March, but traveled slowly and reached the Orinoco in the rainy season. By then his party was decimated. Those who were left built boats and descended the Orinoco, following the river until they were blocked by a waterfall, at which point they were attacked by Indians. In September, 1591 Berrio and a few survivors managed to reach Trinidad. His searching days were over. But he retained his title, because the dream of El Dorado was not yet finished.

In April, 1593 Berrio's lieutenant, Domingo de Vera, took up the search. He was led on through terrible jungles by Indian reports that a great lake or a rich city lay just ahead. (It was always just ahead.) Eventually his exhausted expedition returned to Trinidad. Vera sent an official account of his journey to Spain. It contained the Indians' reports of a fabulously wealthy city in the Orinoco jungles. On its way to Spain the document fell into the hands of one of Sir Walter Raleigh's captains. And with Raleigh we come to the final phase of the El Dorado dream.

Raleigh's Tragic Dream

Raleigh probably first heard of El Dorado from Pedro Sarmiento de Gamboa, a Spanish seaman who was captured and imprisoned by the English and held in London from 1583 until 1588. By Raleigh's time the legend had grown in details. The city of Manoa was definitely situated in a high, cool, more pleasant region of the jungle. The Indians there were not naked savages, but well-clothed, well-fed natives who used gold coins in their daily business. One interesting feature of the story is that they fought only with javelins. And now the Gilded Man was a descendant of the Inca who had escaped from Peru.

Sir Walter Raleigh. His futile search for El Dorado cost him his son's life and eventually his own.

In 1594 Raleigh sent Jacob Whidson to Guiana as the captain of a reconnaissance ship. Whidson's report and Vera's more imaginative one were enough to arouse Raleigh's enthusiasm and in the spring of 1595 he was at Trinidad, ready to find El Dorado. As an English pirate in Spanish waters, he raided Trinidad and captured the aged Berrio. The Spaniard, Governor of El Dorado, was another source of information, and even though there was little that Berrio had to say that was really true, his stories of Manoa and the enormous Lake Parima thrilled Raleigh. However, when Raleigh said he was off to find El Dorado, Berrio spoke differently. He was, in Raleigh's words, "stricken into a great melancholy and sadnesse and used all the arguments he could to disswade me."

The Englishman was not dissuaded. He sailed from Trinidad with high hopes and arrived at the Orinoco, like so many before him, in the rainy season. Before he had gone very far upriver, his expedition was cut short by the arrival of the Spanish. In all, he spent only thirty days on this first search. If he had not found an Indian guide, Raleigh later wrote, "we might have wandered a whole yere in that labyrinth of rivers, yer wee had found any way, either out or in."

His enthusiasm was not dampened by difficulties. He merely noted in his diary: "it is time to leave Guiana to the sunne, whom they worshippe, and steare away towards the North." His diary is not the most reliable of documents. Instead of leaving, Raleigh went on an unsuccessful pirate raid. And he continued to talk to Berrio and others about El Dorado. He heard about a tribe above the Caroni River "whose heads appeare not above their shoulders." One of his informants said he had actually seen these strange people. We recognize them as familiar inhabitants of Neverland.

The dream of El Dorado stayed with Raleigh. Back in England he wrote *The Discovery of the Large, Rich, and Beautiful Empire of Guiana*. Its subtitle is significant: *with a Relation of the Golden City of Manoa, which the Spaniards call El Dorado, etc.* We can see how the legend has grown in Raleigh's account, but how the significant details have remained the same as in the first account the Spaniards heard. The ceremony takes place at Manoa, not at Lake Guatavitá, and it involves an emperor, his governors and captains, and other notables. But the Indians still strip and have their bodies covered all over "with a kind of white balsamum." Then others, "having prepared gold made into a fine powder blow it through hollow canes upon their naked bodies until they be all shining from the foot to the head." The festivities that follow have also been expanded in Raleigh's account. The Indians, sometimes hundreds of them, sit around drinking for six or seven days.

It is remarkable how some details of the legend remained fixed considering that no known person had ever seen the ceremony. Of course, convincing details are the secret of every storyteller's success. Raleigh threw into his book the headless Ewaipanomas, adding more details than in his diary account. They are, he wrote, "reported to have their eyes in their shoulders and their mouths in the middle of their breasts." These creatures straight out of Pliny; the great inland sea of Parima and the city of Manoa all appear on a map prepared by Théodore de Bry in 1599.

Raleigh sent out one of his captains, Lawrence Keymis, to continue scouting the Orinoco. Keymis did some exploring, but kept away from a newly built Spanish fort at the junction of the Orinoco and Caroni Rivers. Then Queen Elizabeth, who protected Raleigh, died, and James I came to the throne. In a gesture to help keep peace with Spain, the new king imprisoned the "pirate" Raleigh in the Tower of London. This did not alter his dream of returning to El Dorado. Raleigh remained in the Tower for thirteen years. When he was released, at the age of sixty-four, he was as ready as ever to find "the Guiana gold." In particular, he wanted to find a fabulous mine that Keymis said he had seen.

Raleigh's second voyage to South America was doomed from the start. He was released from the Tower in March, 1616. By November his plan to return to El Dorado was known in England and probably in Spain as well. His ship, *Destiny*, was launched in December, but he did not arrive off South America until late 1617, after a bad voyage. He found only one comfort in the whole affair. More than twenty years before he had made such a favorable impression upon the Indians that "my name hath still lived among them!" It was small comfort, however, and Raleigh grew more disheartened every day. He remained at Trinidad and stayed aboard his ship.

The exploring was left to Keymis and Raleigh's son, Wat, who went looking for the fabulous mine. Very early on they engaged in an attack on the Spaniards. Wat Raleigh "was unfortunately welcomed with a bullett which gave him no tyme to call for mercye to our heavenly father for the sinful lyfe he had ledde." And from that unfortunate point on everything was downhill.

Keymis explored some more, but was ambushed by the Spaniards and Indians and lost too many men. When he returned to Trinidad, Raleigh blamed him for Wat's death and the failure to find the mine. Keymis locked himself in his cabin and committed suicide by stabbing and shooting himself. There was nothing left for Raleigh but to return home. King James was delighted to order his execution to please the Spanish ambassador. And when Raleigh went to the scaffold in 1618 El Dorado died with him.

The End of El Dorado

Like other Neverlands, El Dorado died hard and left lingering ghosts. These geographical phantoms remained because El Dorado was sought in a region that was difficult to explore. The presumed site of El Dorado was actually the world's largest rain forest, an area of constant rain, straddling the equator, perpetually clouded by its own steaming heat. A breeding ground for all sorts of diseases, it was filled with swamps and populated by poisonous snakes, piranhas, insects, and unfriendly natives. Few regions on earth, even today, are as inhospitable to man and none has ever been as unlikely a spot for Neverland.

The ghosts of El Dorado lingered on. Lake Parima was a feature on maps at least until 1800. Between 1800 and 1802 the famous naturalist Baron Alexander von Humboldt explored seventeen hundred miles of jungle to disprove its existence. Meanwhile, Spanish engineers attempted to drain Lake Guatavitá, where the legend began. The job was finally accomplished in the twentieth century by a party of English explorers. They found some gold objects at the bottom of the lake, of archaeological interest but certainly not a fabulous treasure.

A popular feature of the legend was a hidden high plateau. This, at least, had some basis in fact. In the Guiana highlands, between the Orinoco and the Amazon, where Brazil, Venezuela and British Guiana meet, stands Mt. Roraima, 9,219 feet high. Long after the search for El Dorado had ended, the hidden plateau remained a romantic geographical fixture. Sir Arthur Conan Doyle used a South American plateau as the setting for his 1912 novel *The Lost World*. There his heroes meet ape men and dinosaurs. At the end of the novel they return to London with a live dinosaur. And that is probably the most that anyone, in fact or fiction, has brought out of El Dorado.

As we have seen, Neverland is always around the next bend of the river, or beyond the next mountain. It lies at the junction of Long Ago and Far Away, in a country of the mind. What we have explored are worlds created by the human mind and heart. We have traveled with heroes and liars, and have seen facts turned into legends and legends turned into facts. Neverland—not fiction, but fancy; not fact, but real; simultaneously imaginary and true; a dream that found its way onto the map.

SUGGESTIONS FOR
FURTHER READING

On Neverlands and fabulous voyages:

Bailey, J. O., *Pilgrims Through Space and Time: Trends and Patterns in Scientific and Utopian Fiction.* New York: Argus Books, 1947.

Cohen, Daniel, *Mysterious Places.* New York: Dodd, Mead, 1969.

de Camp, L. Sprague and Will Ley, *Lands Beyond.* New York: Rinehart, 1952.

Furneaux, Rupert, *Myth and Mystery.* London: Wingate, 1955.

Ley, Willy, *Another Look at Atlantis.* Garden City: Doubleday, 1969.

On early travelers and the world picture:

Crone, G. R., *Maps and Their Makers: An Introduction to the History of Cartography.* London: Hutchinson, 1962; paper, Capricorn Books, 1966.

Herrmann, Paul, *Conquest by Man.* New York: Harper, 1954.

Leithauser, Joachim G., *Worlds Beyond the Horizon.* New York: Knopf, 1955.

Morison, Samuel Eliot, *The European Discovery of America: The Northern Voyages* A.D. *500–1600.* New York: Oxford, 1971.

Penrose, Boies, *Travel and Discovery in the Renaissance, 1420–1620*. New York: Atheneum, 1962.

For classical references:

Graves, Robert, *The Greek Myths*. Baltimore: Penguin Books, 1955.

Harvey, Sir Paul, ed., *The Oxford Companion to Classical Literature*. Oxford: Oxford, 1937.

Seyffert, Oskar, *A Dictionary of Classical References*, rev. and ed. by Henry Nettleship and J. E. Sandys. New York: Meridian Books, 1956.

For more on specific subjects:

Ashe, Geoffrey, *Land to the West: St. Brendan's Voyage to America*. New York: Viking, 1962

Ashe, Geoffrey, et al, *The Quest for Arthur's Britain*. New York: Praeger, 1968

Donnelly, Ignatius, *Atlantis: The Antediluvian World*, rev. ed. New York: Gramercy, 1949.

The Travels of Marco Polo, trans. Ronald Latham. Baltimore: Penguin Books, 1958.

Mavor, James W. Jr., *Voyage to Atlantis*. New York: Putnam, 1969.

Miller, Helen Hill, *The Realms of Arthur*. New York: Scribner's, 1969.

Naipaul, V. S., *The Loss of El Dorado*. New York: Knopf, 1955.

The Buke of John Maundeville, ed. Sir George Warner. London: 1889.

INDEX

Arculf, Bishop, 68
Argo, 22, 23, 26–27, 32
Argonautica (Apollonius of Rhodes), 21
Argonauts, voyage of, 19, 21–26, 29, 42, 43
geography of, 27–33
map, 29
Argos, 22
Aristotle, 87, 110, 113, 127, 132
Arrian, 80–82, 91
Arthur, King, 61, 150–54, 170, 171, 179
Arthurian legend(s), 17, 150–73
development of, 154–58
Glastonbury and the Holy Grail, 168–73
and historical Arthur, 150–54
other Arthurian places, 166–68
popularization of, 158–60
and search for Camelot, 160–66
Ashe, Geoffrey, 61, 62, 63
Assyrians, 87
Atalanta, 22
Atlantica (Rudbeck), 133
Atlantic Ocean, 37, 41, 42–43, 53, 61, 95–96, 130
Atlantis, 12, 13, 16, 110, 125, 127–49, 190
conflicting theories about, 136–38
in Critias, 130–32
Donnelly's theory, 138–43
growth of the legend, 132–33
Lemuria and, 135
Lyonesse as, 163
map, 141
Minoan Crete and, 143–49
modern theory, 143–49
and Mu, 133–35
origins of story, 127–29
and Tartessos, 136
in Timaeus, 129–30
Atlantis: The Antidiluvian World (Donnelly), 138
"Atlantis Not a Myth" (E.H. Thompson), 134
Atlas, 130
Atlas Mountains, 130
Aurelius Ambrosius, 155, 156
Australia, 114

Avalon, Isle of, 157, 159, 160, 167–68, 169, 171–72, 173
Azores, 53, 63, 96, 140

Babylonians, 86, 87
Bacon, Sir Francis, 132, 138
Bacon, Roger, 104
Badon, Mount, Battle of, 152, 154, 166
Bahamas, 62, 63, 64
Bailly, Jean Sylvain, 133
Balaklava (Crimea), 40
Baltic Sea, 30
Barka Kahn, 70
Bath-Hill (Mons Badonicus), 152, 157
Batum, 30
Bede, Venerable, 152, 153, 155
Bedivere, Sir (Bedwyr), 158
Belalcazar, 194, 195
Berrio, Antonio de, 197–98, 199, 200
Bible, 17, 172, 180
Bicherod, Janus Joannes, 133
Bilad Ghana, 191
Bimini, 9
Black Cathay, 177
Black Sea, 23, 28, 30, 31, 32, 37, 41, 44, 80
Blavatsky, Mme. Helena P., 135
Blessed, Fields of, 110
Blessed Isle of the Celts, 109
Blessed Isles, 107, 108–11
Blessed Souls, Island of, 168
Boccaccio, Giovanni, 40
Bodel, Jean, 157
Boeotia, 28
Bojador, Cape, 191
Borneo, 50
Bors, 169
Bran, voyage of, 54–55
Brasseur, Abbé, 134
Brazil Rock, 13, 53
Breasted, James H., 115
Brendan, Saint (The Navigator), 13, 47, 52, 53, 57, 64, 84, 109, 119
and geography of Atlantic Ocean, 61–66
legends related to, 54–61
map, 56, 65
Britain, 106, 108, 119, 120

398
Fri   Frimmer, Steven

        Neverland

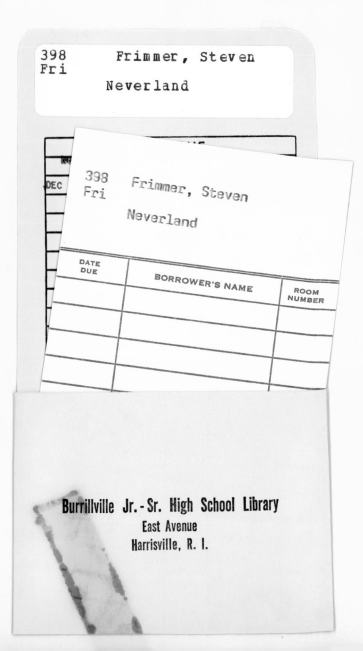

398
Fri   Frimmer, Steven

        Neverland

DATE DUE	BORROWER'S NAME	ROOM NUMBER